skunk girl

SHEBA KARIM

skunk *girl*

FARRAR STRAUS GIROUX

NEW YORK

www.fsgkidsbooks.com

Library of Congress Cataloging-in-Publication Data
Karim, Sheba.
Skunk girl / Sheba Karim.— 1st ed.
p.   cm.
Summary: Nina Khan is not just the only Asian or Muslim student in her small-town
high school in upstate New York, she also faces the legacy of her "Supernerd" older
sister, body hair, and the pain of having a crush when her parents forbid her to date.
ISBN-13: 978-0-374-37011-4
ISBN-10: 0-374-37011-7
[1. Interpersonal relations—Fiction.   2. Pakistani Americans—Fiction.   3. Family
life—New York (State)—Fiction.   4. High schools—Fiction.   5. Schools—
Fiction.   6. Muslims—Fiction.   7. Dating (Social customs)—Fiction.   8. New York
(State)—Fiction.]   I. Title.

PZ7.K1422 Sku 2009
[Fic]—dc22

2008007482

For Faisal

skunk girl

The *Keera* in My Brain

'm a giant in the sky flying over crimson-roofed houses, dressed in a wool turtleneck and jeans. It's hot and I've started to perspire, a fine drizzle of sweat that falls onto the village below. That's when I see a group of elves walking single file. They're carrying hot fudge sundaes, lots of whipped cream and no cherry, just the way I like them. As I'm about to swoop down and attempt to steal a sundae, someone grabs my shoulder. It's a ghost, and it knows my name. "Nina."

"Nina." The ghost is still gripping my shoulder. My mother. Her hair is tied tightly back and nearly every inch of her face is covered in white cream bleach.

"Wake up, *beta*," she says. Her fingers smell like onion and chili powder; she's already made breakfast. She always likes me to start the school year off on a full stomach. "It's your first day of school!"

She says this as though I should be excited. Though it is indeed the first day of my junior year of high school, none of the feelings swilling around in my head bear any relation to excitement. In fact, they're pretty much the opposite of excitement. After spending much of the summer reading the two SAT prep books my parents had bought me, it's easy to come up with possible antonyms. Unenthused. Disinterested. Reluctant.

My mother shakes her head. "Sonia was always so excited to start a new year of school, but you never want to get out of bed."

I sit up. "I'm awake now, Ma. Happy?"

"I made you an omelet," she says. "Hurry up before it gets cold."

And so I rise, and so begins another year. Another year of social exile, another year of not fitting in, another year of not measuring up to the legacy left by my sister, Sonia, another year of wishing I were someone else, someplace else. Who on earth would be excited about that?

My father's in the kitchen and extends his arms out wide as soon as he sees me. I brace myself. He's a small man, but bearlike in his affections, often testing the capacity of my lungs to withstand intense pressure in the form of zealous embraces, though as I've become older, the duration of these embraces has lessened. "Nina!" he booms cheerily, squeezing me for a second before letting go. It's a rare moment when my father isn't in a merry mood. If we were white and Christian, he'd be one of those dads who dress up as Santa Claus every Christmas. "Ready to ace calculus?"

"I'm not taking calculus till next year, Dad," I tell him. His forehead furrows. Sonia, of course, started calculus in her junior year, which is probably why he looks so confused.

"Don't worry, you will be soon!" he says, as if calculus were some major milestone every teenager aspires to achieve.

My father has no surgeries scheduled at the hospital this morning, so after we eat my mother's omelets he offers to drive me to school, which is fine with me since I don't have my license yet and it's embarrassing to be seen stepping out of a yellow school bus when you're a junior in high school.

As soon as we get in the car my father puts on his favorite kind of music, *qawwali*, Sufi mystical music. Sometimes, when he gets really into it, he sings along and does this gesture with his right hand, like he's unscrewing a lightbulb. But today he stays still. It's a little too early in the morning for musical theatrics, even for my father.

We drive past rows of houses with small yards and swing sets and the occasional inflatable pool, and stop at the light in front of the old roller rink, which was shut down a few years ago and has been abandoned ever since, weeds and shattered glass blanketing the steps to the entrance. Back in 1986, when I was in fourth grade, this roller rink was the epicenter of the social scene. I used to hate having wheels on my feet. When I did go roller-skating I'd hold on to the wall that bordered the rink as the other kids raced by me, skating hand in hand, or backward, or both. Mostly when I went I sat around with my friends Bridget and Helena, and sucked on red and green ice pops, the kind wrapped in plastic that you squeezed from the bottom up.

We take a left and then a right onto Main Street. The words "Welcome to Deer Hook" are painted across the brick wall of a store, also abandoned, which is next to another abandoned store, which is next to the offtrack betting parlor, where already there are a few old men in stained clothing loitering outside, the necks of liquor bottles sticking out from the paper bags in their hands. Deer Hook's Main Street has a bad half and a better half, divided by the main intersection, the only intersection on Main Street that has a traffic light. We cross the light into the better half and I can tell you the order of what we pass without looking: the movie theater, the Italian restaurant La Traviata, the

Ming Dynasty Chinese takeout place, the pizzeria, the taxidermist shop with the stuffed moose head in the window. I've spent my whole life in this town and nothing here has really changed, except for some businesses shutting down and never reopening, like the roller rink. In this town, things aren't reborn or reinvented. Everything that doesn't stay the same either dies or goes away.

For as long as I can remember I've pretty much hated Deer Hook, population 11,250. When I was in middle school, I had a game that I liked to play. I would close my eyes and touch a globe ever so lightly with my finger. Then I'd spin it with my other hand. Wherever my finger landed when the globe stopped spinning was where I was going to end up living, and I would yell out the name of my future home. "Australia! Egypt!" If it landed on someplace like Kansas or an ocean, I cheated and spun it again. "Brazil!"

One day, my father walked in as I landed on New Zealand. "New Zealand!" I shouted.

"What are you doing?" he asked. I explained. My father raised his bushy eyebrows. "You have a *keera* in your brain," he told me. *Keera* is the Urdu word for "insect." What my father meant was that I had something in my brain that was giving me strange ideas, like wanting to live halfway across the globe. This was a bit hypocritical, considering he had moved halfway across the globe, but I didn't mention this, because he would have said, "That's different." Instead I imagined the *keera* in my brain. He was a friendly-looking insect, like a cricket, with big, powerful green eyes that could see the world beyond Deer Hook, beyond Albany and New York City, all the way to New Zealand.

My father pulls into the circular driveway in front of Deer Hook

High, a U-shaped one-story building with a statue of Henry Hudson in front of the entrance. There's a ton of people milling around, talking and laughing, most of them familiar. Huddled together by the statue is a group of nervous freshmen. "Have fun!" my father says. My fingers tighten around the door handle. Once I exit this car, there's no going back. It's not that I hate high school, it's just that I wish it would hurry up and end already. But I suppose to understand this, you have to understand the story of my life thus far. The dread I'm now feeling is a culmination of years of dealing with things that end in "shun," at least phonetically: repression, suppression, exclusion.

My name is Nina Khan, and growing up, there were two things that especially plagued me. The first was my sister.

League of the Supernerds

Sonia was a supernerd. By the age of three, she had taught herself how to read. She would spread *The New York Times* on the floor and lie down in front of it, propped up on her elbows.

When my parents' friends, whom I call aunties and uncles even though they're no relation to me, saw Sonia with the newspaper, they'd say, "Oh, how sweet. She's pretending to read the paper."

On cue Sonia would run her finger along the page and start to read out loud. "The Dow Jones Industrial Average fell 10.6 points on Friday . . ." The aunties and uncles were astonished. My mother and father beamed.

For years and years to come, my mother would tell the story of how Sonia, at the age of four, asked her who Dow Jones was and why he was so often falling.

Ha ha ha.

When I was born, everyone waited to see if Nina would join her sister in the ultraexclusive League of the Supernerds. They were soon disappointed. I didn't even start talking, really, until I was almost two. I had to sit through all of first grade, whereas Sonia, who was multiplying and dividing in kindergarten, skipped right over it.

In seventh grade, Sonia received a 1410 out of 1600 on her SATs, and got to take special classes every Saturday. I had a hunch that these "classes" were really secret meetings of the League of the Supernerds, where they discussed how, after making life difficult for their younger siblings, they would take over the world. On Saturday afternoons, Sonia, my mother, and I would drive an hour to Albany to drop Sonia off at her class. Then my mother and I would go to a nearby mall and sit in the food court for two hours. My mother would read magazines in Urdu and I'd eat fish sticks smothered with tartar sauce. Then we would pick Sonia up. I'd watch from the car as the supernerds tramped out of the building. They weren't the most attractive bunch, lots of shaggy hair and thick glasses and pale skin. Some of them even squinted when they walked outside, like they were unaccustomed to the sun. It must not have required much physical strength to take over the world because I was only eight and I probably could have beaten up a lot of them.

As soon as she got in the car, my sister would open up a book. She was always reading a book, and she always carried a few extra in her book bag for backup. And every Saturday, after my sister opened up her book, I would make a request of her. "When you take over the world, can you give me an ice cream factory?" I asked. Sometimes I asked her to make me a movie star or a detective or to rename Niagara Falls "Nina Falls" after me. No matter what I asked for, Sonia just looked up and shook her head, giving me a "duh" look.

One Saturday, I asked her, "When you take over the world, can you make me white?"

When I said this, my mother hit the brakes and turned around. "Why would you want that?" she asked. This time Sonia didn't look up from her book.

Because it sucks being one of the only brown kids in school, I thought. But I didn't say this because even then I knew my mother wouldn't understand.

Red, Black, and Blond

When I get out of the car I find Bridget and Helena sitting on the steps to the left of the group of frightened freshmen. Bridget, Helena, and I have been friends since first grade. We are nothing alike. Bridget is tall, with dirty blond hair, and has long appendages that sometimes knock into people and objects. Though she can be clumsy on foot, she's extremely graceful on skis. Helena is petite and blessed with the kind of color palette that prompts a double-take—fiery red hair and aquamarine eyes. She is a hopeless romantic and a card-carrying optimist. And then there's me.

"Nina!" Helena cries. "It is *so* good to see you!" When Helena says such things, she really means it. "I have to tell you about my summer."

"Let me guess," I say. "You fell in love."

She blushes. "I wanted to write you letters and tell you all about it, but you told me I couldn't." The reason she couldn't send me letters is because my mother has little regard for the fact that opening someone else's mail is a federal offense, and if she ever sees mail addressed to me she'll open it without thinking twice, and the less my mother knows about my friends' love lives, the better.

"Allow me to bring you up to speed," Bridget says. "She had a torrid affair with this guy named Pete who was also a camp counselor."

"We only had six weeks together, but, in a way, that was what was so wonderful about it. The idea that there was a definite end in sight made each moment we did have together so passionate. I've never felt such emotional intensity in my life." Behind Helena, Bridget rolls her eyes at me. "Stop rolling your eyes, Bridget," Helena says without turning around. "One day you guys will understand what I'm talking about."

"Yeah, when the devil puts a snow cone machine in hell," Bridget retorts. While Helena has had a steady line of boyfriends since eighth grade, Bridget's love life thus far has consisted of a few awkward hookups.

"Oh, I totally understand what Helena's talking about," I say. "I also had a torrid summer romance—with my SAT book." Bridget snickers and Helena shakes her head.

"Just wait, Nina, until you find love," Helena says.

"Yeah, that'll happen the same day Deer Hook turns into a cosmopolitan, ethnically diverse metropolis," I say, and take off before Helena tries to convince me that love is just around the corner. For me, turning a corner at Deer Hook High offers no promise of possibility. It just means I'm that many steps closer to a class I won't do as well in as Sonia.

After my English class, I've got precalculus. Mr. Gagen is our precalculus teacher, but everyone calls him Mr. Porcupine because the hair on his head is short and sticks straight out in clumps as if he put his hand in a socket. He lectures us about radian and degree measures, and I take lots of notes. It feels good to be learning about something new after weeks of memorizing vocab words and the definitions of mean, median, and mode.

At the end of class, Mr. Porcupine stops me on my way out. "Nina, can you stay for a minute?" I walk up to his desk. "I was thinking of your sister the other day. How is she doing at Harvard?"

"Sonia's good. She likes Harvard a lot."

He's hunched over, the needles on his head pointing directly at me. "She was my very best student."

I am silent.

He sits back. "But I'm sure you'll impress me too."

"I don't really like math," I tell him. This is a lie—I like math well enough—but there's no point in giving him false hope. Nina is not Sonia. As I leave the classroom I realize I can say this in different languages. *Nina no es Sonia. Nina n'est pas Sonia. Nina Sonia nahin hai.*

The End of Sleepovers

My freshman year was the year that everything really changed. When I started high school, not only was I the lowest of the low in a literal sense, but I had the looks to match. I was overweight and still had braces. In the summer between eighth and ninth grades, my hips became too round and my thighs too mushy. Parts of my body jiggled when poked. The one thing that stayed small were my breasts—A cup and so far apart from each other I had to squeeze them together with force to get any cleavage. Not that I was allowed to show cleavage anyway.

My friends had a much better freshman year than I did. High school is easy for bubbly redheads like Helena. Back then, she had braces on her teeth, but everyone thought they looked supercute on her. Helena was recruited by practically every extracurricular club. She can't do a split to save her life but still got onto the cheerleading team, and when she quit after the first practice because physical exercise isn't really her thing, the cheerleaders told her she would be dearly missed. Bridget joined yearbook and, of course, the ski club, which was full of athletic boys with names like Josh and Carl who said hello to her in the hall, raising her cool quotient by at least two degrees. I debated joining yearbook too, but decided I didn't want to join a club whose sole purpose was to memorialize the awkwardness of our lives, and joined the Volunteer Society and the French club instead.

I've always been one of the youngest people in my year, which means that by the time I experience a rite of passage, everyone else is already acting blasé about it. Almost all of the girls in my class got their period in eighth grade and seemed to know so much more about life because they could debate which brands of pads were more absorbent. I, of course, didn't get my period until the first week of freshman year. It happened in the middle of French class. Finally, I thought, *je suis* a woman.

When I got home and told my mother, instead of congratulating me or crying like my friends' mothers had, she informed me that I could no longer sleep over at my friends' houses.

"But that's not fair!" I had been sleeping over at my friends' houses for years. "I can't sleep over because I got my period?" My mother had her back to me, and if she did hear me, she pretended she didn't. "I don't understand."

My mother turned to face me, her lips pressed together tightly. Whenever my mother becomes upset, she makes her lips disappear. Then she wrapped her hand around the onion she had been peeling and waved it in the air. Sometimes, when she's trying to make a point she thinks may be contested, she'll make a fist around something and shake it, dictator-style, as if my social life were some banana republic she has complete control over. "Because your American friends will start doing things you're not allowed to do."

"If I was a boy would you do the same thing?"

"It's not the same. Girls can get pregnant. But yes, I would. Nina, you know things are different for you. You're a Pakistani Muslim girl."

"So what?" I said, even though further discussion was futile. There was nothing I could say, no arguments I could make, that would trump the fist followed by the Pakistani Muslim girl statement. I could have cried for days or banged my head against the wall, but it would have been of no use.

The good Pakistani Muslim girl my mother wants me to be does things like the following: speaks fluent Urdu, fasts during Ramadan, wears *shalwar kameez*, enjoys going to boring parties with other Pakistani families where the kids sit in the basement watching a movie while the aunties and uncles talk and laugh upstairs. But sometime in middle school, I began to want to do all of the things good Pakistani Muslim girls didn't do, like wear short skirts and flirt with boys. Sometimes I would imagine what the Pakistani Muslim girl my mother was referring to must look like. She had long black hair and eyeliner in a thin, perfect line across her lids and was always smiling. But in her head I was sure she was thinking, *God, I am so bored I just want to stab myself in the chest and end my miserable life.*

I've never been to Pakistan. Even though my parents have talked about going almost every year, we've never gone. Except for my mother's only sister, Nasreen Khala, and her family, all of our relatives have moved elsewhere, to Canada and Dubai and England, and at least once a year these relatives will come visit us, various aunts and uncles and cousins. On the first day of the visit they make weird faces at me as I stumble over my Urdu and then give up and speak English, and after that I try to speak to them as little as possible.

Nasreen Khala is the worst. Every time I answer her questions she looks down at me, double chin and all, and shakes her head slightly like she feels sorry for me because I am so Americanized. This is one of Nasreen Khala's favorite words; she uses it a lot when she visits. "Children here are becoming so Americanized." She'll always pause before saying "Americanized" and pronounce it "um-ree-can-ized." I could say, "Yeah, well, you're fat and have BO," but of course I never do. I would get into a lot of trouble for not respecting my elders and it would just give Nasreen Khala even more proof that I was umreecanized.

Thankfully, most of the relatives who come to visit never stay for more than a few days, since there's nothing to do in Deer Hook. At some point during their visit we pile into the minivan early in the morning with coolers packed with sodas and quart-sized Ziploc bags full of snacks—samosas and *pakoras* and *chewra*—and make the long drive to Niagara Falls. I usually have to sit on the floor in the back with the little kids. We admire the falls and take a million pictures and go on a boat ride and then drive all the way back home, and within the next day or two my relatives leave and I can open my mouth and speak again without feeling nervous.

Wild African Ass

Principal Young announces that for the first week of school we're allowed to eat lunch on the lawn behind the gym, as some kind of special treat. Even outside, the cafeteria groupings apply. Most of the black kids and the handful of Latino kids sit in one area while the white kids take up the rest of the lawn. The few other minorities, like me and Steve Chang, a freshman whose parents own Ming Dynasty, sit on the white side. It has to be the hottest week in the history of Deer Hook, and all of the girls at school are wearing tank tops and short skirts that show off their freshly shaved legs. I'm in jeans. "Aren't you hot?" Bridget asks me. I am but I don't say so. My legs are sweaty and my jeans feel like they're papier-mâchéd on. I think of the women in the desert countries of the Middle East who wear black burqas, and I wonder how they manage. The students of Deer Hook High wouldn't know what to make of those women. They think I'm weird for wearing jeans when it's sweltering out.

"Vinny Henderson asked me out this morning," Helena says.

"What happened to Mr. Camp Counselor?" Bridget asks.

Helena tilts her head, a wistful "isn't life wonderful" smile spreading across her face. "Pete was an incredible guy, but we both knew it was only a summer romance, and the summer is officially over," she says. "Besides, he lives in Maryland." Helena can afford to move on so readily because she's never lacking in suitors; the first day of school is barely half over and the boys are already pursuing her.

As if to underscore this, there, above us, is the sound of Shannon Kelly's voice. "Hello, gorgeous." I don't bother looking up from my turkey sandwich; he isn't referring to me. Shannon has had a crush on Helena for years. Unfortunately for him, he's the only boy in school shorter than her, and he's also annoying. He used to approach me during kickball games in elementary school, tapping his hand repeatedly over his open mouth, Native American–style. "Is that how you speak at home?" he would ask. "I'm not that kind of Indian," I'd tell him. "What are you, then?" he'd say. I wanted to explain that I was born on one of the four floors of Deer Hook Hospital, next to the Shady Pines Nursing Home and across the river from the junkyard, just like he was. "I'm not that kind of Indian," I'd repeat. "I'm not even Indian at all." But he never stuck around long enough to listen.

"How are you, Helena?" Shannon asks.

Helena smiles up at him and his face starts turning the same shade of red as his Irish freckles. It amazes me how Helena can turn boys into bumbling fools merely by adjusting the curvature of her lips. "I'd invite you to sit down, but Nina was about to tell us something that's kind of private. You know, girl stuff," she says.

Shannon squints at me, as if I'm sitting at a distance instead of right in front of his face. I wonder if I should clap my hand over my mouth a few times so it's easier for him to recognize me. "Okay," he mumbles. "I'll catch you later?"

We watch him walk away, fists jammed deep into his pockets. "Do you have to use me as the excuse?" I ask. "Can't you use Bridget once in a while?"

"It's easier to use you. You're more mysterious," Bridget says.

"Why? Because I've never been spotted at a party? Anyway it's not like most of these people haven't seen me practically every day for years."

"High school is different," Bridget says. "You're no longer Nina, the girl who used to suck at kickball, but Nina, the possessor of two boobs that none of the boys have ever seen."

"What is that supposed to mean?" The thought of any of these boys looking at my breasts creeps me out and I cross my arms in front of them.

"Can you two stop being so crass?" Helena says.

Serena is heading our way so I put my sandwich down and wipe my mouth with my napkin, lest Serena catch me with mayonnaise on my face. If I were ever to have a nemesis, Serena would be it. She's a blonde, blonder than Bridget, and has one of those button noses. Her parents own a game farm and because of this and her cute nose she's never been lacking in friends. Each year from second through fifth grade she'd have her birthday party at the game farm. Her parents would close the farm to the public for the afternoon so Serena and her friends could have the whole place to themselves and feed the baby goats for as long as they wanted. I've never been invited to Serena's birthday parties. Whenever Serena runs into me in school, she wrinkles her nose for a second as if I just farted.

"Hi, Serena," Bridget says. Bridget is friends with Serena; their parents are old friends and Serena and Bridget have been hanging out together since they were babies. Serena is always nice to Bridget and Helena. They claim that I exaggerate Serena's cruelty, that since we started high school she's never done anything outrightly mean to me, which may be true, but if a disdainful expression speaks a thousand nasty words, then Serena has given voice to an entire encyclopedia of degradation.

"Girls." Serena pauses. I assume she's doing this for effect, since she already has our full attention. "I have some very exciting news."

"Do tell," Helena says.

Serena kneels down between Bridget and Helena. She's wearing a tight baby blue tank top that says "Deer Hook Game Farm" in pink letters. In the center of the shirt is a picture of an animal that looks like a donkey. Of course Serena would wear her ass on her chest. "You know how I always ask my parents if I could host a party at the game farm and they always say no because they think some high school kid might get drunk and do something stupid?"

"That's because some high school kid would get drunk and do something stupid," Bridget points out.

Serena ignores this. "Well, last week I managed to convince them to let me have one. It's going to be the best party of the year. I've decided to invite every single person in the senior and junior classes, and a few select sophomores and freshmen." Great. Serena has finally included me on her guest list, and I won't be able to attend. "The party's next weekend and I'm giving out actual invitations," Serena continues, removing a stack of envelopes from her bag. "I got them from our gift shop—they're Shetland pony cards. So adorable, right?" She hands one each to Bridget and Helena and waits for them to ooh and aah, which they do. "We are going to rock the game farm like it's never been rocked before," she declares.

"It sounds like fun!" Helena exclaims.

Serena looks at me. "Nina, I'd give you one, but Bridget told me you're not allowed to go to parties anymore and I don't want to waste any. That's okay, right?" She blows a big pink bubble. Serena is fond of bubble gum, mostly the pink kind, and is always getting yelled at by our teachers for it. She sucks the bubble back in. A piece of it sticks to her upper lip and she picks it off with a long fingernail.

"It's okay," I say. If the world of high school is a cell, my friends and all of the other students are in the nucleus, and me, well, I'm floating in the cytoplasm, close to the nucleus but not quite a part of it. Mostly, I've been okay with this. I can't participate in a lot of the activities that are supposed to make high school socially exciting, namely, boys and parties, but I don't like any of the boys here, and I don't really want to hang out with anyone from my school except Bridget and Helena anyway. Still, once in a while, like when Serena is prancing about handing out "actual" paper invitations to a party that's going to "rock the game farm like it's never been rocked before," suddenly the cytoplasm starts to feel lonely and suffocating.

"Do you realize you're going around wearing an ass across your chest?" Bridget asks Serena.

"If you look closely," Serena says, stretching out her tank top so we can read the name of the animal written in small italics underneath the picture, "it's not just any ass, it's an African wild ass, and it's one of the rarest mammals in the world. In fact, when you come to my party you can see one in the flesh." When she says "flesh" I swear she's looking right at me, and my insides start burning. One glance from Serena can make me so self-conscious and uncomfortable in my own skin. Every time she looks at me, imperious blue eyes over impetuous button nose, I feel like she can see through my clothes, right to the source of my shame. Because, as annoying as my sister has sometimes made life for me, she pales in comparison to the second plague of my life—body hair.

Gorilla

Now, of course it didn't happen overnight, but that's what it felt like, and that's how I remember it.

One morning freshman year I woke up and was covered in hair. The hair was in varying degrees of thickness and density; thick hair on my legs from my thighs down to my ankles, hair that's less thick running down the length of my arms, soft hair on my stomach and in the space between my breasts. I'd had some hair on my upper lip for a while, but that day it was suddenly fuller and darker, a proper mustache. There was hair on my toes and my fingers and the sides of my neck.

I fell asleep a human, and woke up a gorilla.

I screamed. I pounded my fists against the mattress. Then I ran to find my mother. She was downstairs making breakfast: omelets with onions and green chilies, *paratas* and *alu bhujia.*

"Look!" I said, holding out my arms. I lifted up my pajama leg to reveal one hairy calf. I pointed to my mustache.

"What?" she asked.

"I'm a beast!" I yelled, collapsing on a chair.

My mother shrugged. "A lot of Pakistani women are hairy, Nina. It's not a big deal."

Not a big deal! *Not a big deal!* What wasn't a big deal to her was reason enough to never leave the house again to me.

"But my arms, my legs. My mustache!" I pointed to each body part as I named it. "Help me," I pleaded.

"Well, no one sees your legs, so don't worry about that." My mother picked up a fork and stirred the omelet mixture with a few expert flicks of her wrist. Then she said, "Follow me."

I followed her to her bathroom, where my mother has two entire drawers full of ninety-nine-cent nail polish in every conceivable shade of brown, pink, red, and purple. Part of her routine whenever she gets ready for a Pakistani party is to examine the entire contents of the drawers and find the nail polish that most closely matches her clothes.

My mother opened the cabinet and pulled out a blue-and-white box. "Here," she said.

I looked at the box. Jolen creme bleach. I had often seen my mother walk around the house with bleach on her face, and once I walked in on Sonia in the bathroom, reading a magazine on top of the toilet seat cover, with bleach all over her face. I didn't know why it had never occurred to me that this too would be my fate. Did I think

I was special? Did I think I would escape the Pakistani hairy gene? I just didn't think about it at all. Stupid me.

"That will take care of your face," my mother said. "It burns a little. Don't keep it on for more than fifteen minutes." She pulled tweezers out of the drawer and handed them to me. "These are for your eyebrows."

I went to my room and read the instructions on the bleach box. Mix the activator into the cream. Apply. Leave on seven to ten minutes and wash off. You were supposed to try a test patch first to see how your skin reacted but I didn't bother. After I spread the bleach all over my face, covering every inch of skin except the area around my eyes, I looked at my ghostlike reflection in the mirror. I felt like I was being initiated into a tribe I didn't want to be a member of, a tribe of hirsute women.

I washed off the bleach and examined myself in the mirror. My skin was blotchy and red, but the hair was now blond and I could hardly see it. Then a ray of sun shone through the bathroom window and lit up my face, illuminating each and every hair. They were still there all right, every single one of them. Even so, blond was better than black.

My parents were already eating when I went back downstairs. "Let's see," my mother said. She put her hand on my chin and turned my head left and right. "Very nice! Don't worry, the redness will go away soon."

"All of the hair is still there though. If the sun hits my upper lip at a certain angle, my mustache lights up like my face just won a jackpot." And there was still the matter of the rest of my body, I thought.

But I knew my mother's response to that. "No one should be seeing your body anyway, Nina," she'd say.

"You know, when I was in college in Pakistan, they didn't sell hair bleach," my mother said. "We had to make it ourselves by mixing ammonia with hydrogen peroxide. It used to burn so much! See how much easier it is now? You should consider yourself lucky!"

"What's wrong with a little hair?" my father joked. Though he had bushy eyebrows and thick black tufts of hair on his shoulders and back, he could get away with it because he was a man. It was acceptable for men to be gorillas. You never saw them spreading Jolen bleach on their shoulders.

Asher

Right when I've decided to bite the misery bullet and endure another boring school year, something happens that changes life as I know it. His name is Asher Richelli.

He's a junior too, a transfer student. He moved here from Buffalo, but spent most of his life in Italy. He can speak perfect Italian and perfect English. He is made of different shades of brown: very light brown skin, dark brown eyes, and medium brown hair that flops and curls. He's six feet tall and has a small gap between his two front teeth. Practically every girl in school falls in love with him at first sight, and I bet even the most popular ones would give up their place on the prom committee or cheerleading team in a heartbeat just to have their fingers tangled up in his hair.

Rumors fly when he appears in school. His parents are Italian royalty on the run for tax evasion and are hiding out in Deer Hook, where no one would ever think to look. Asher Richelli is not his real name. His family is not royalty, but part of the Mafia. He was born in the Italian Alps and is a champion skier. Soon the truth emerges. He was born in Pisa, then moved to Buffalo awhile back, and now his parents have taken over the Italian restaurant on Main Street. He works there on weekends.

I always liked math, but the day Asher Richelli enters my precalculus class, it becomes my absolute favorite subject. I'd seen him in the morning at his locker down the hall from mine, and have been waiting for another sighting, and now here he is, in the flesh, moving in my direction. Asher walks between the rows of desks with ease, like he has no worries at all, like he doesn't care or maybe doesn't even realize that people are watching him. He takes the seat behind and diagonal to me and I picture what I must look like from that angle. My hair is a mess, as usual. I've never been able to style it; I can't blow-dry it straight or crimp it or curl it properly so I leave it wavy and long, the ends turned out in different directions. Maybe Asher is noticing how wide my hips are. Or maybe he's noticing the long strands of hair that sweep around each side of my neck. Or how the backs of my arms jiggle. Or, more likely, he's not noticing me at all. I turn around to see whether this is true or not, and our eyes meet.

"Hi," he says. "I'm Asher."

"Nina," I say. My heart is pounding so hard I feel like it is going to leap out of my chest and land on my precalculus book, still beating.

"I bet you're the smart one in the class." He smiles wide, revealing all of his teeth.

"Asher Richelli," Mr. Porcupine says. "Where were you the first week of school?"

Asher makes this cute throat-clearing sound. "I was in Italy for a wedding," he replies.

I was in Italy for a wedding. It sounds so adult, so worldly. I realize that I've been waiting my whole life for someone to walk into one of my classes and say this exact sentence. And, just like that, I have a sense of purpose. I now officially live and breathe to catch another glimpse of Asher's smile, to admire that glorious little gap between his teeth.

Bellissima

My crush on Asher grows at warp speed, and within days it occupies many of my thoughts and all of my daydreams. Shakespeare is meant to be heard, according to Ms. Tazinski, our English teacher, and one day the junior English classes meet in the auditorium. Everyone takes turns reading parts from *Romeo and Juliet*. Asher reads the role of Romeo for a few pages. He pronounces Signor Martino and Vitruvio and Placentio in his Italian accent and it makes my skin hot. After class I can hear some of the girls trying to mimic his accent to their friends, but of course it's stripped of its beauty coming out of their lip-glossed mouths.

Asher's been here almost a week, but we haven't spoken since his first day. He only nods his head at me whenever he sees me in the hall or in precalculus. This does not bother me. My love can feed on looks alone. What worth have words anyway?

But a battle rages inside me, between the realist and the romantic. The realist says there is no way Asher will ever like me, that I am unattractive and hairy and uncool and even if he did want to ask me out, I can't go on dates and everyone knows that. The romantic says he could appreciate my lovely eyes, light brown with a subtle ring of green around the iris, and imagines a secret romance, fueled by meaningful looks and passed notes and stolen kisses in the school parking lot.

At night, when I close my eyes to sleep, the realist is banished and the romantic has free rein. I picture Asher confessing his love for me after precalculus, taking my hand and pressing it against his cheek. I imagine him taking me to dinner, a table for two on the terrace of a villa overlooking fountains and orchards. He feeds me tiramisu with an ornate silver spoon, an heirloom that has been in his family since the sixteenth century. "The legend is that whoever you feed with this spoon will be yours forever," he whispers, leaning toward me. *"Bellissima,"* he says, and we kiss. Oh, how we kiss.

One day, in history class, I make a list.

Why Asher Would Like Nina
I am funny
I have nice eyes
I am kind
My braces are off and my teeth are now straight
I am intelligent but not a supernerd
I have a passport
I can make spaghetti with meat sauce
~~Like him, I am exotic~~

I cross out the last one because I am not exotic like him. I don't have a cool accent and European good looks. According to the students of Deer Hook High, I am exotic in the same way Chinese people eating dog is exotic—a bad way. After I make the list I tear it up into little pieces. I can't take the risk of anyone in school or my parents finding it. The first would mean ridicule; the second would mean endless lectures and even more restraints on my social life. But, even as I'm shredding the list, I'm daydreaming—I accidentally drop the list on the ground and Asher finds it and chases after me to tell me that he does, indeed, like me, for all of the reasons I wrote down, and for some I hadn't even thought of.

Serial Killers

All week, everyone at school has been talking about Serena's party: who's invited, what they're going to wear, who's going to sneak in the alcohol, if some drunk person might accidentally open the door to the monkey cage. Pretty much everyone is going, including Asher. Everyone except me, of course.

I spend the night of Serena's party at home with my parents, watching television. We watch a show about detectives trying to track down a serial killer who lures women into his car, kills them, cuts them up, puts their body parts in shopping bags, and then leaves these bags in garbage cans around the city. "So many evil people in the world. I wish I could keep you with me always," my mother says, putting her arm around me. "And never talk to any strange men on the street or get in anyone's car!" Duh. Then she remembers she has a daughter who lives on her own in a city that could be teeming with serial killers. She picks up the phone and calls Sonia. It is ten-thirty on a Friday night. Sonia doesn't answer.

I wonder what Asher is doing at Serena's party, who he's talking to, if he likes animals, if he thinks the party is fun, if he realizes I'm not there. I wish I was there, where I could be flirting with the boy of my dreams. But I'm never *there*. Instead, I'm here, sitting on the couch in between my parents.

My mother calls Sonia a half hour later. Still no answer. "Where is she?" I take this as a rhetorical question and don't respond.

"Look, they caught the serial killer," I say. The detectives are walking him to the police car. He's a skinny white guy with big, square glasses that have slipped to the tip of his nose, but he can't push them up because he's handcuffed. Then they interview people who used to know him. One woman has bleached blond hair tied back in a tight, high ponytail. "He was a loner in high school, always real quiet, never came to any social events," she tells the camera. This makes me think maybe there are only two types of people who spend their Friday nights in high school at home—Pakistani Muslim girls and future serial killers. Though I suppose Indian and maybe even some Asian parents might be as strict with their kids. My father mentioned that an Indian family moved to Deer Hook and they have a daughter in middle school. Maybe I should become friends with her. I bet we'd be allowed to spend our Friday nights together, memorizing vocabulary words or something.

My mother calls Sonia again at eleven-thirty, and then at midnight. No answer. Now she is pacing around the kitchen. My father is sitting at the table eating leftover chicken *biryani* with his hands.

"How can you eat?" she yells at him. "Our daughter could be dead!"

"Sonia would never get into a strange man's car," my father says, taking a big bite. That's my father, always positive, always trusting, and always able to eat. At dinner he always has two huge helpings, covering every inch of his plate with food. He is five feet seven and thin, and I can never figure out where the food goes. Sonia inherited his metabolism, but I take after my mother, whose every bite heads straight for her hips and thighs.

My mother is praying on her favorite prayer rug, the one that has blue and black flowers and depicts the Kaa'ba, the holiest shrine in Islam, in the center. "I promised Allah I would perform ten *naafil* prayers if Sonia is okay," she informs us when she's done. She folds over the top corner of the rug before getting up. When I was little I asked her why she did this and she said if you don't fold the corner then Shaitaan can stand on the prayer rug and start mocking Allah. I still don't understand why this simple gesture would stop the devil from standing on the prayer rug. Maybe he has a phobia of folded corners.

At one a.m., Sonia answers the phone. "Sonia!" my mother cries. "I was worried about you! Why were you not in your room? You shouldn't be out at this time of night. It's dangerous!" My mother listens for a minute, then says, "The library is open so late on Fridays? Are you sure it's safe to walk home from there at such an hour?"

I head upstairs. The walls of my room are pink and I sleep in a canopy bed. I made my father take down the canopy freshman year, but the four poles remain. I wonder if Asher is still at Serena's party. There must be girls all over him, hanging on his every word, begging him to speak to them in Italian. Serena's probably right in there with them. I picture Serena's smirk, the horrible, mocking one she seems to reserve especially for me, and my stomach clenches. It's not her fault I can't go to her party, but it feels good to have something to channel my discontent toward. I imagine Serena falling into the elks' cage at the game farm. I imagine the baby goats feeding on her. What a tragedy, everyone would say. Such a pretty girl. Eaten alive by elks and goats. All that was left of her were little bits of pink bubble gum, stuck to the bottom of the cage.

Wish It Were Sunday

It must be masochism Monday, because as soon as Bridget and Helena and I sit down for lunch I say, "You guys have hardly told me anything about the party," though I'm really directing this statement at Bridget, who can usually be relied upon to tell it like it is, even if it's not what you want to hear.

"You didn't really seem interested on the phone," Bridget says, "so I figured you didn't want to know."

"My mind is officially inquiring," I tell her.

Bridget shakes her head. "It was a real scene. They were playing hip-hop music over the speaker system, and everyone was dancing. Serena's parents and some of the employees were there to make sure things didn't get out of hand. Shannon Kelly snuck in beer inside his backpack, and Vinny Henderson followed Helena around all night, and then Vinny almost got into a fight over Helena, and Helena told Shannon to get lost—"

"I would never say it like that," Helena protests.

"And then Shannon went away all mad and somehow managed to pour beer into the bottles they used to feed the baby goats, and the goats got tipsy, and when her parents found out they called off the party. Serena was so pissed." Bridget manages to say this all in one breath, and concludes by knocking over her milk carton with her elbow.

"Those poor goats!" Helena says, handing Bridget some napkins. "How can people be so cruel to animals?"

"How can Serena be so cruel to humans?" I ask.

"Do you ever think you might be acting a little cruel toward her?" Helena is eating a celery stick and it's making her eyes look green. Her eyes can change color, from blue to green to everything in between, depending on what she's wearing or what she's eating or her mood. "She's not such a terrible person, Nina, really."

I ignore this. "Was Asher there?"

"Yeah," Bridget says, "though you could barely see him through the throng of girls that surrounded him everywhere he went."

I put my hands over my ears. "I've heard enough."

"Yes, enough," Helena says.

"So what's up with you and Vinny anyway?" I ask her. "Are you two really dating?"

"Sort of. But I got a letter from Pete," she answers, lowering her voice.

"I thought it was only a summer romance," Bridget says.

"It was. He just wrote me to say hello and reminisce about the summer. It was so sweet. He wrote that my hair rivals the sunset." Bridget sticks her finger in her mouth in mock disgust. I situate myself somewhere between Helena and Bridget on the cheese-tolerance scale. I wouldn't mind receiving a letter from Asher that says my hair rivals a sunset. "The point is," she continues, "that Vinny is a nice guy, but he would never write me a letter like that."

"That's because he can barely write," Bridget says.

I cover my mouth so Helena can't see me smiling, but you can tell even Helena finds it funny; there are deep dimples in the center of her cheeks because she's sucking them in, which she does whenever she really wants to laugh but thinks it would be rude.

"He can write, thank you very much. Anyway, I have to give Vinny a chance. Don't laugh—there's something so fragile about him. He's like a wounded bird. He needs someone to help him heal."

The rest of the day I think about how, in my own way, I am also a wounded bird who longs to fly with the others but can't. I wish Asher could see this and save me like Helena plans on saving Vinny, except in order to save me he'd have to get me a new set of parents who'd allow me to date. Then, when I get home that night, my mother dabs some salt on my wound. "Guess who's coming to visit?" she says.

Great. That's just what's been missing from my life lately, some random relative coming to visit and making me feel culturally inadequate. "Who?"

"Nasreen Khala."

Oh, joy. Between the picture I have in my head of Asher being followed by a cattle of oogling girls at the game farm and the news that my aunt who disapproves of how umreecanized I am is coming to town, this day can't get much worse. But I can't let my mother see how unenthused I am. Nasreen Khala is her dearest relative, and she always looks forward to her visits. "That's great," I say, and head up to my room. I have designated tonight as a leave-no-root-unripped waxing night, and there is much work to do.

Next Stop: Street Hooker

I run into precalculus class right as the bell rings. There is Asher, in his usual seat diagonal from mine. And then it happens. As I walk down the aisle Asher winks at me. A real eye-completely-closes-then-opens wink. My heart starts to race and for the rest of class I debate the meaning of this wink. Was it a "hey, how's it going" wink, or a "you're late for class, you naughty girl" wink, or a "I think you're kinda cute and this is my immature high school way of saying it" wink? In any event, for the first time I feel as though Asher and I have communicated on a new level. Smiles to winks is a definite progression. What will be next? Actual talking? For the remainder of the period, even though I can see Mr. Porcupine's lips moving, I can't process anything he's saying. Things are happening. I must seize this opportunity, be bold and confident. I must talk to Asher at the end of class.

The bell rings. I develop a sudden case of paralysis from the neck down and stay seated at my desk, glancing over my shoulder once at Asher, who's gathering his books and doesn't notice. As he walks by me I smile and say—nothing. I don't even open my mouth. So much for bold and confident.

That night, my mother works on some billing while my father and I eat dinner. My mother has a rule that though she'll sit with us, she won't eat until all of the work she needs to do for the day is finished. My mother studied accounting in Pakistan and was going to apply for a master's degree, but then my parents moved to Deer Hook and she became the office manager/accountant of my father's cardiology practice, which as far as I can tell consists of endless calculations and paperwork.

"Why don't you eat and finish later?" my father says.

My mother glares at him. "These have to be in by the end of the week or we'll miss the deadline for reimbursement." She shakes her head. "Without me this practice wouldn't even make half the money it does."

"That's true," my father agrees. "Keep working."

My mother throws a giant paper clip at him and he tickles the bottom of her chin with it and she smiles. I like it when my parents are cute like this. It makes me happy that they found each other, or, rather, that their parents chose them for each other.

The phone rings and my father gets up to answer it, his mouth full of food, as usual. He was one of five children and they used to treat dinner like some kind of race. He still eats as though he's competing for the finish, making big pyramids of rice and dal and meat with his hands and stuffing them into his mouth.

"Hello?" My father pauses, then he swallows and says, "You want to speak to Nina? Who is this?" in a strange, slightly accusatory tone, the only explanation for which is that there must be a boy on the phone.

Could it be Asher? He somehow understood that I was too shy to talk to him in class so now he's taking the initiative! What am I going to do? What am I going to say? My heart has turned into a Russian gymnast, leaping and swinging about the parallel bars that were once my rib cage. Oh, Asher! My parents are both staring at me. Oh, no.

"Robbie? Hold on." My father puts his hand over the earpiece. "It's a boy named Robbie from your school. He wants to talk to you," he says to me in Urdu.

It must be Robbie Nash. He's the overzealous president of the Volunteer Society and is probably calling to order me to do something for it.

My mother and father are silent, watching as I take the phone.

"Hello?" I say, turning away from my parents.

"Hi, it's Robbie."

"Hi, Robbie." I'm trying to sound normal, but it's hard with my parents sitting right there, gearing up for the inquisition. You stupid idiot, I want to yell, do you have any idea what this phone call is going to cost me?

"I'm organizing the bake sale next week and I need to know what you're bringing. You were supposed to tell me by the end of school yesterday and you neglected to do so, in spite of me reminding you twice."

Robbie used to be a quiet, unassuming kid, but whatever authority being president of the Volunteer Society gives him has completely gone to his head. "Um, I'll make brownies," I say, twisting the phone cord around my wrist.

"I'd prefer that you make Rice Krispies treats. We already have two people making brownies."

"Fine. Rice Krispies treats it is."

"And you should put something fun in them," he adds. "Like chocolate chips or M&M's."

"Yes, all right," I say, convinced that there is now a hole in the back of my shirt that my parents' eyes have burned through.

"Well," Robbie says, "which of those do you think you'll put in them?"

"It'll be a surprise. I gotta go." I hang up the phone.

When I sit back down my father says, "Who was that?"

"It was Robbie Nash, you know, the president of the Volunteer Society. He wanted to see what I was bringing to our bake sale," I say.

"That's all he wanted, right?" my mother asks, and the lips start to disappear.

"Yes! Why, do you think I'm lying?" My voice cracks with anger. It's ridiculous that I can't even have a one-minute conversation with a boy about a bake sale without being interrogated.

"You need to calm down, Nina," my father says through his food.

"Sonia never got any phone calls from boys and she was involved in many extracurricular activities," my mother says.

"And what if I told you that he was one of my friends? What is the big deal about having friends who are boys?"

Now it's my father's turn. "Nina, I know it is not easy to hold on to your Muslim values in this society, but if you lose sight of what is right and what is wrong, and start behaving like Americans, you'll end up on the streets, on drugs, and a prostitute." My father is serious when he says this. Whenever he talks about what will happen if I let go of my Muslim values I always end up being a street hooker on drugs. It is so preposterous that you can't even argue with it.

My mother reaches out and ruffles my hair. "We know you're a good girl," she says.

Right now I feel so many things, sad and guilty and angry and, yes, a little proud, but most of all, I feel like a fraud, like a good Muslim girl impersonator. Welcome to my life, the teenage masquerade.

Behind the Reptile House

The witch took me shopping," Helena tells Bridget and me at lunch.

The witch is Maria, Helena's father's girlfriend. Helena doesn't always apply her rule of seeing the best in everyone to her own family. Her parents got divorced when she was seven. They fought over custody and it got pretty ugly and her mother ended up letting her father keep Helena and left Deer Hook for good. I remember Helena crying one day in school and telling me her parents were getting divorced, and I started to cry too, because she looked so sad. Then I went home and asked my mother what *divorced* meant. She explained what it was and told me that, after death, it was the worst thing that could happen to a family. "But don't worry," she said, "it won't happen to you as long as you listen to your mother."

"Did she buy you anything nice?" I ask. Maria, with her stilettos and silk blouses, is the best-dressed woman in Deer Hook, or the most overdressed, depending on how you look at it. Helena's father met her last year when he was flying to California for business. She's a flight attendant and isn't around that much, which is fine with Helena. When she and Helena's dad first started dating, Maria would bring Helena gifts: perfume from Montreal, pure maple syrup from Vermont, a box of taffy from San Francisco. Then, after she moved in with them, the gifts stopped and Maria, a former high school beauty pageant contestant, started telling Helena that she should take aerobics classes and eat grapefruit and melba toast for breakfast and that she shouldn't leave the house without mascara, all things Helena doesn't appreciate hearing.

"She's already asking me what I'm going to wear to prom. She kept talking about how great prom was in her high school, how they would have it at a hotel, and Deer Hook is such a dump it doesn't even have a proper hotel. She's always putting Deer Hook down, like she's too good for it and she's stuck here because of my father. Just like my mother." Helena pauses. "Anyway, we went to the mall, and then she keeps trying to get me to buy this pink dress. And I keep telling her I don't wear pink because it makes me look like a tomato, and she laughs and says, 'Everyone loves Italian.' I swear, that woman thinks she is so entertaining. I ended up buying a black dress. She hates black." She pushes her lunch tray aside. "All right, I'm done complaining. Let's talk about something else. What's up with you, Nina?"

I scrape the meat off my taco and start breaking the shell into little pieces. "I tried to talk to Asher yesterday and I chickened out like a coward."

When I say this, Helena and Bridget exchange a look. "What?" I ask.

"You haven't heard?" Bridget asks.

"No. What?"

"Serena asked Asher out after her party and he said yes."

First clarify, then panic. "What do you mean by yes? Yes, I consent to have a meal with you, or yes, I like you too and would absolutely love to go to dinner with you?"

"Neither one, probably, but more the latter than the former, I think," Bridget says.

I accidentally hit my tray and bits of taco shell cascade onto my lap. "Are they, like, *going out*?"

Bridget shrugs. "Who knows? Serena was all over Asher at her party, and they disappeared together somewhere behind the reptile house for a good half hour and even went out the next night, so I think they're on the road to coupledom."

"I cannot believe you didn't tell me this before," I say.

Bridget folds her arms and twists one long leg around the other. Her body always becomes more pretzel-like when she feels defensive, as though if she twists herself into knots she'll be better protected from the sting of accusation. With some practice, Bridget could probably join the circus as a contortionist. "I was going to tell you before, but then you put your hands over your ears and said 'enough' and Helena was kicking me under the table so I didn't."

"I didn't want you to get upset," Helena pipes up.

"Why didn't you tell Serena not to ask him out?" I demand. "Why didn't you at least discourage her?"

Bridget sighs. "What would I have said? 'Listen, Serena, Nina really likes Asher and even though she can't ask him out and can't even talk to him you're not allowed to ask him either'? Asher's not your boyfriend, Nina. He's not even your friend. You can't claim him."

"That's not the point," I snap, but of course, that is exactly the point. Bridget is only stating the ugly truth. I have no claim over Asher. Asher's so cute that I knew it wouldn't be long before he started dating some girl, a girl who would not, could not, be me. But for him to go out with Serena? Stupid, hateful button-nose bubble-gum Serena? I can just see them at the party, Serena wrapping herself around him like a boa constrictor. "I have to go." I get up and head for the door, leaving a trail of taco bits behind me.

At the end of the day, Bridget is waiting for me in front of my bus. "Hey," she says.

"Hey."

"Listen, I'm sorry I didn't tell you about Serena before. Helena thought we should break the news to you gently, but I should have known better than to follow Miss Softie's advice. It must really suck for you that Asher is dating the girl you hate."

"I don't hate her," I say. "I just can't stand her. Anyway, you were right, it's not like I could have asked him out anyway."

"I know," Bridget says. "It's so hard for you, not being able to do anything." She looks at me, all sympathetic. I feel like one of those kids you see in magazine ads that you can save for the cost of only one cup of coffee a day. But she's missing part of the point; it isn't just the not being able to do "anything," it's also watching your two best friends doing everything right in front of you, moving on in ways that you can't.

"It's okay," I tell her.

"Listen," Bridget begins, but instead of continuing she twists her arms around each other.

"I'm listening . . ."

"I think I like someone."

"You do? Who?"

"I don't want to say yet. I feel like that could jinx it."

"Big-mouth Bridget keeping a secret from us? Is it possible?"

"Can you be serious for one second? The problem is I want to ask him out, but I don't think I can do it. Every day I'm like, today is the day, I am Bridget, hear me roar, but every day I chicken out. It's so embarrassing—I can ski down a double black diamond without flinching, but I'm totally wimping out on this. Why is this dating thing so frigging easy for people like Helena and Serena and so hard for me?"

If Bridget didn't look this tormented, I'd smile at the fact that she's asking the girl who's even more chicken than her for advice. "Bridget, you never have problems stating your mind and you shouldn't with this either. The worst thing that can happen is that he says no, right? You can do it, girl. And if you can't do it for yourself, do it for me. Do it for your friend who couldn't ask out anyone even if she wanted to." This angle seems to be working, because Bridget has untwisted her arms and started nodding.

"Yeah," she says. "I'll do it for you."

"For us." I salute her.

Bridget starts laughing. "You're a freak, but I'm glad we're friends."

I can never stay mad at Bridget for long, because even though she sometimes talks before she thinks, she's still Bridget, the klutzy girl who accidentally spilled red fruit juice down the front of my white dress at our elementary school graduation, then intentionally spilled the rest on herself so I wouldn't be the only one covered in juice. "Me too," I say, and as we hug I hear Shannon Kelly yell, "Look at the lesbos!" to the great amusement of everyone around us.

Pol Pot

When I come downstairs for dinner my mother is on the telephone with Sonia. "Do you want to talk to her?" she asks me.

I shake my head. If Sonia and I had the kind of close sibling relationship propagated by Hallmark cards, I might take the phone and go up to my room and tell her that even though I know it's crazy, I feel that Asher has somehow betrayed me, and she would offer sympathy and sisterly words of advice, but we barely even have a relationship. And I don't think Sonia knows much about boys. She definitely didn't care about them in high school. The only boy she ever talked about was Vithu Duong. She talked about him a lot, not because she had a crush on him but because he, as the only other supernerd at Deer Hook High, was her archrival.

Vithu's parents came from Cambodia as refugees. My sister was the only South Asian girl in high school and Vithu was the only East Asian. They were both National Merit Scholars, and they took turns winning pretty much every academic award offered in the entire region. Each night at dinner Sonia would give us a play-by-play of the latest round in the Sonia versus Vithu academic death match, followed by analysis and commentary, such as, "Vithu got a perfect score on our calculus test. I missed one question, about the derivative of a vector. But East Asians usually excel at math, so I am totally operating at a genetic disadvantage."

Sonia and Vithu were the only people at Deer Hook High who applied to Harvard and Yale. Half of their class didn't even apply to college. Then, as Sonia was preparing her applications, the guidance counselor told her that Harvard and Yale often wouldn't accept more than one student from small high schools like Deer Hook High. When Sonia heard this, she started to freak out. She stayed up at night thinking of ways to make her application better than Vithu's. She told me that at school the students were taking bets on who was going to be valedictorian, she or Vithu, and more people had bet on Vithu. "Misogynists," she called them.

One day, she looked like she had been crying. At dinner, she asked my mother, "Are you sure you and Dad aren't refugees? Is anyone in our family in political exile? Did you and Dad overcome dire poverty or any other great obstacle to come here from Pakistan?"

"You know the answer, Sonia," my mother said. "We both came from middle-class families."

My sister groaned. "Vithu is writing his college essay about how his parents escaped the Khmer Rouge. There is no way I can beat that! I am not going to get into Harvard or Yale, all because of stinking Pol Pot." She put her head down on the table.

I didn't know who Pol Pot was, but he didn't ruin my sister's life like she thought he would because in the end, Sonia and Vithu both got into Harvard and Yale. And Cornell and Brown and Stanford and MIT.

But the point is that there is no point in talking to my sister about a boy. She'd just tell me to forget about him and go study so I can get into Harvard like her.

Where They Belong

It hasn't even been a week since Serena's party and already Serena and Asher are acting like a full-fledged couple. I saw them this morning, walking down the hall together, occasionally pausing to say hi to someone. The whole time Serena kept shifting. As I watched them I realized there's a method to her shiftiness; the reason she continually repositions her body is to ensure that her boobs remain right under Asher's nose. Her scheme seems to be totally working; Asher kept eyeing her chest. It's a shame I can't put Serena in a burqa.

I'm the first one at the lunch table. From where I'm sitting I can see Helena and Vinny, who are on their weekly lunch date. They're another pair who recently got together and quickly transitioned into a full-fledged couple. It's like everyone's gotten hooked on some kind of relationship amphetamine. Helena's talking a lot and Vinny's nodding and kissing her in places like her shoulder and her ear and each time he does this Helena pushes him away gently. If Asher and I were to fall in love, we would not engage in such idiotic activities. Instead, he would spend the lunch hour reading aloud love poems he had written for me. First, he'd read them in Italian, and then he'd translate them for me. The girls in the cafeteria would blister with envy, Serena most of all.

My daydream is interrupted by the appearance of Bridget, who looks like she's on some kind of drug herself, her face flushed and a little sweaty. "So I asked him out and he said yes!" she exclaims.

It takes me a second to figure out what she's talking about. "Hooray! Now will you please tell me who it is?"

"Anthony Ames."

"Anthony Ames? *Schwa* Anthony Ames?" When I hear his name, two things come to mind—schwa and biceps. In seventh grade, Anthony Ames became obsessed with schwa, the upside down *e*, and he wore a green sweatshirt with a black schwa on it every day for weeks. Then, freshman year, he became a workout buff, and now has biceps the size of mangoes. "Are your parents going to care?"

"I don't think so," Bridget replies. The reason her parents might care is because Anthony Ames is black. "But I guess I'll find out when I tell them."

"Why Anthony?"

"I think he's so sexy," Bridget says. "I've had a crush on him since last spring."

I shake my head. "Who are you? You're usually so bad at keeping secrets." I still can't believe this whole time I've been going on about Asher, Bridget, of all people, has been keeping her own adolescent love longings under wraps.

"I know," Bridget says. "I guess it's not easy for me to talk about my romantic feelings."

"Is there anything else you've been hiding from us?"

"Nothing. Only that." She leans across the table. "Nina?" she whispers. "Do you think he'll like me back?"

"Of course he will. How could he not?"

"I don't even know him that well," Bridget says. "What if we have nothing to talk about?"

"You'll find something to talk about. And if you don't, then just stick your boobs in his face like Serena was doing with Asher today."

"If I had any, I would." Bridget is even more flat-chested than me, but, unlike me, she has great legs, especially her glutes, which are strong and curvy from years of skiing.

"What do you think your parents will say?" I ask.

Bridget shrugs. "My parents like to think they're enlightened, but who knows? Although my dad does go golfing a lot with Mr. Hutchinson." Mr. Hutchinson is the town's most successful black resident. He owns a small department store called JJ Hutchinson's. His daughter was in the same class as Sonia and received one of the Deer Hook High academic awards for seniors, the only one not given to either Sonia or Vithu.

"I'm sure your parents will be fine," I tell Bridget. And then I see my future—Helena and Vinny on a lunch date in one corner of the cafeteria, Bridget and Anthony in another, and me, still at the same table we've sat at throughout high school, alone, staring woefully at some bruised piece of fruit.

"Are you okay?" Bridget asks.

"I'm fine," I say, and force a smile. I don't want her to think that I'm anything but happy for her, because that's what friends do, support one another on their path to happiness even if it could make life a little less happy for them.

"Don't worry," Bridget says. "Even if I do start dating Anthony, I am never going to be gross like them." She points at Helena and Vinny, whose heads are pressed together. "Oh, Helena," she mimics Vinny's raspy voice, "I am a poor, wounded sparrow."

"My wing, it's broken and I can no longer fly," I add.

"And the only way to heal me is for you to suck face with me," Bridget says.

"Please don't be so crude with Anthony in the beginning. Like Helena would say, maybe you should break yourself to him gently."

Bridget shrugs. "He's either going to like me for who I am or he isn't. And if he doesn't like me, he can go to hell." She tucks her hand under her armpit and makes a farting noise. She's really good at it and it drives Helena crazy. She doesn't have to put on this show for me, but it's good to practice. In high school, a little bravado can go a long way.

"I bet people like Heather Esposito would have some kind words to say about an interracial relationship," I say.

Bridget shrugs. "Who gives a crap about Heather Esposito? I barely talk to her."

As I walk to class I think about Heather Esposito. In middle school, she fascinated us for a number of reasons: she had the most beautiful singing voice in our class ("Like a cherub," Mrs. Havermeyer, our chorus teacher, said) and got to sing most of the solos in chorus, and she was graceful and athletic and had the fiercest kick of any girl in kickball. In fifth grade, she kicked the ball so hard at Greg Peabody's head that he fell down, and then he had to repeat fifth grade because of the brain damage, or at least that's what Heather told everyone.

Then, one day in sixth grade, Heather Esposito came to school with a bruised lip and a missing front tooth and refused to tell anyone how she lost it. Finally, after Helena begged and offered her the homemade cupcake from her lunch, Heather told us. "A black guy robbed me on the street and punched me in the face. All of the black people should go back to Africa and live with the lions because that's where they belong. That's what my father says."

We were silent. Then, after a minute, Helena said, "That's racist. You shouldn't say things like that."

"Yeah," Bridget added.

"But it's true." Heather shrugged and held out her hand. "Gimme the cupcake."

I remember I couldn't sleep that night. I kept wondering if Heather had ever said anything like that about me, that I should go back to Pakistan and live with the monkeys because that's where I belonged. As the only minority in the group, I should have been the one to speak up. But it was easier for Helena to do that kind of thing. She didn't have to worry about antagonizing the racist. She already was where she belonged.

The Antonym of Me

Serena is in my English class. She usually sits way on the right and I usually sit way on the left, but today I get to class late and the only open seat is directly in front of her. She wrinkles her nose at me. "Hi, Nina."

"Hi," I say, and quickly face the front, but she, for some reason, decides she wants to talk to me.

"It's too bad you couldn't come to my party," she says. "It's definitely going to be one of those high school parties everyone remembers years from now, you know?"

I half-turn around. "Yeah, I heard it was a lot of fun." My stomach churns in anticipation of whatever comment or look Serena may give me that will make me feel self-conscious and unattractive. Talking to Serena causes its own kind of nausea.

"It was awesome. Well, next time I host another large event maybe you'll be able to come," she says. Just like her, to rub my nonlife in my face. "I was telling Asher how I want to have another party at the game farm, but my parents said now that they'd seen what teenagers could actually do to a place, they'd never allow it again, and he said, 'Your parents have a point, Buttons.' That's his nickname for me. 'Buttons.' Asher is such a cutie-pie. Don't you think?"

I offer a weak smile. "He's quite a pie."

"He's the best kisser," she whispers.

That's it. After having to witness visual reminders of their relationship every day this week, these verbal reminders, direct from the horse's mouth, are the final straw. I must get over Asher. What is the point in pining away after a boy who goes for the breasty blonde—the antonym of me? I may as well pine after a Hollywood celebrity.

Ms. Tazinski walks in. "Nina, face front," she says. "Serena, please spit out that gum immediately."

I try not to think about Asher for the rest of the day, but as soon as I lie down to sleep he's all I can think about: his face, the spot on his left cheek where he always forgets to shave, the way the gap between his front teeth gets a little narrower at the bottom, the zit on the very tip of his chin that he's had since last week. If Asher and I were dating, would he have a nickname for me? I'm not sure what it would be, but it'd be so much cooler than Buttons. That much I'm sure of.

There Is a Light That Never Goes Out

Saturday night. Bridget is on a date with Anthony, Helena is on a date with Vinny, Asher is on a date with Serena, and I am on a date with fried foods and Morrissey. I'm in my room, blasting a Smiths mix tape I made last summer and singing along as I polish off a bag of salt-and-vinegar potato chips, when there's a knock on my door.

"What!" I yell, not touching the volume.

"Can I come in?" my father yells back. He hardly ever bothers me when I'm holed up in my room—that's my mother's domain.

I shut off the music and open the door. "What is it?" I ask him.

"What does it have to be to let me in your room?" he says, and then laughs. He laughs at his jokes more than anyone else does, but I have to give him an A for effort, and sometimes I laugh along with him.

"Does Ma want something?"

"No. She's watching a Pakistani drama," he says, and steps into my room. He doesn't come in here much, so after he enters he looks around with a lot of interest, like he's in a museum or something. He picks up the tape cover. " 'The Queen Is Dead and she left me this mix tape,' " he reads. "Who killed the queen?"

"You did."

He looks confused.

"Oh, never mind," I say.

He sits down on the bed next to me. I wait for him to make some joke, but he's quiet for a while, tapping the bedpost as I count the white spots on my fingernails. Then he says, "You know, I bought my practice from Dr. Schmidt."

Not only is it rare for my father to be in my room, but he has replaced his jovial manner with a more serious demeanor. "I know," I say.

"And some of the patients who had been going to Dr. Schmidt refused to see me after I took over his practice. They didn't want to go to a foreign doctor. They would drive an hour out of their way so they didn't have to be treated by someone who wasn't white. I was offended at first, but I got over it. These people felt how they felt, I could not change that. And, in the end, my practice did fine without them."

I realize that I have never given much thought to the difficulties my parents must have faced after moving here. "Way to be strong, Dad," I tell him.

His hand hovers above mine for a few seconds as though it's wondering whether it's safe to land, and then descends, squeezes my wrist, and returns to his lap. He still doesn't say anything, but keeps making these half-nodding movements with his head, like he's encouraging me to do something. I wonder what it is he wants me to do and then I realize that he wants me to open up to him. It's the "I confide in you then you confide in me and then we embrace" scenario. He wants us to have a *moment* like they do in TV sitcoms. But there aren't any TV sitcoms about rebellious Muslim teenagers and their parents, and if there were I bet the audience would be laughing *at* us, not with us.

"Dad." I'm about to say that I am tired and want to go to bed, but it's only nine o'clock, and part of me feels guilty. I mean, it is sweet that he's reaching out to me, especially since we hardly ever talk about anything personal. But if I were to tell him the truth, that I've fallen for an Italian boy, it would be the last moment we ever had because I'd be shipped off to Pakistan to be "un-umreecanized," which would probably involve a lobotomy.

"What is it, *beta*?" my father asks. "You've been spending so much time in your room. Is there something bothering you?"

"It's just bad PMS," I tell him.

My father nods and his jaw moves like he's chewing on something. He's now entered teenage-girl-menstruation-icky-zone and isn't quite sure what to do. He rubs his bald spot with his index finger. "So I've been thinking about shaving my head. Do you think I'll look chill with a shaved head?"

"Not chill," I correct him. "Cool."

"Cool," my father repeats, and starts laughing. I start laughing too, and I want to hug him, tell him I love him, thank him for trying, but I haven't told him I love him since I was a little girl, and it feels too weird to start now.

"Hungry?" my father asks, and even though I just ate, I say yes. The two of us head down to the kitchen and start taking leftovers out of the fridge. I put on a Nusrat Fateh Ali Khan tape and we sit across from each other, tapping our feet to the *qawwali* music and eating rice and dal and *keema*. Maybe it didn't turn out to be the father-daughter moment he was looking for, but I have to admit it's kind of nice all the same.

The Great Sinkhole

I've been assigned bake sale duty during fourth period on Monday. Robbie Nash has written detailed instructions on a piece of paper, in case we couldn't figure it out ourselves. "Make sure to give customers exact change." "Ask them if they would like a napkin." I'm debating whether or not I should cross out "napkin" and write "slap in the face," when I hear Asher's voice. "Hey, Nina."

Asher is in front of the table, surveying the goods. He must have snuck out of gym class because he's in mesh shorts and a T-shirt. I'm glad we have gym on different days, so he can't witness my utter lack of athletic ability. "Quite a spread," he says. "Did you make any of these?"

"The brownies," I blurt out. "No, not the brownies. I meant the Rice Krispies treats."

"Wow. They look really great," he says, as if a Rice Krispies treat could have an aesthetic. "I'll take one."

"They have M&M's in them," I say, a little too enthusiastically, as I give him back his exact change. He smiles and I tell myself to stop behaving like a five-year-old child. But still, he could have bought anything, a brownie or a cupcake or an oatmeal raisin cookie, but he chose to buy my Rice Krispies treat. Could this mean something?

By lunchtime I have decided that before I read anything into Asher's bake sale purchase, I should first obtain the latest Asher-Serena-status update from Bridget. I'm sure Serena has called her over the weekend to exchange date stories. "So what's up with Asher and Serena?" I demand as soon as I sit down. "Give it to me straight."

"You sure?" Bridget asks. Helena tries to flash her a look, but I put my hand in front of her face.

"I can handle it," I say.

"If you say so." Bridget takes a deep breath, then spills it. "They decided they're officially a couple."

It couldn't be worse, but I can't say I'm surprised. Helena rests her head on my shoulder. "You okay, Nina?"

"Yeah, I expected as much." Oh, Asher, you traitor. "Now tell me about your dates."

Bridget cocks her head to one side and smiles. Super. Another friend lost to the great sinkhole called love. "It was awesome. Anthony is really cool, and really funny. I think I spent the whole night laughing. I can't wait for you guys to get to know him."

"Bridget and Anthony and Vinny and I are going to the movies Friday," Helena says to me. "Come with us. Please."

I can't decide if it's better to be a fifth wheel than to be no wheel, so I tell her I'll decide later and head to class, pondering what might have been. It's a futile exercise, but an oddly comforting one, since no one can ever prove you wrong. If I had asked Asher out before Serena did, would he have said yes? Or would he have laughed in my face? In this realm of conjecture, I allow myself a fifty-fifty chance, which may be the best odds I'll ever have.

Fifth Wheel

The rest of the week passes uneventfully; besides saying hello, Asher and I don't speak. I think of asking how the Rice Krispies treat was, then I see him and Serena arm in arm and figure bringing up his purchase would only tip the scales further against me in Serena's favor—Serena = sexy, well-endowed woman; Nina = girl who won't shut up about juvenile baked goods.

Friday night is so warm and pleasant it feels like the beginning instead of the end of September. I'm standing in the lobby of the Main Street movie theater with Bridget and Anthony. Only one movie is shown here at a time. It used to be a real theater and it still has a stage and red velvet curtains that are drawn back to reveal the screen. Bridget keeps squeezing Anthony's arm, and I would too, if I were dating him; he's so ripped he could probably lift Bridget over his head with one hand. But though his body is totally cut, he still has a baby face, his cheeks almost as chubby as they were when he was a kid, a dime-sized bit of fat protruding from the tip of his chin.

"Bridget's told me a lot about you," Anthony says, shaking my hand, which is oddly formal considering we've gone to school together for years.

"Like what?" I ask.

"She told me that you were the one who ran into the boys' bathroom in third grade and screamed 'Fire!' I remember I was about to take a leak and I got so startled I peed my pants."

"That was Bridget!" I protest.

55

Bridget laughs. "But you dared me to."

"I really liked those pants," Anthony says, and Bridget punches him in the arm.

"Probably not as much as you liked that schwa sweatshirt," I joke.

Anthony nods. "I loved that sweatshirt."

"Yes, we know!" Bridget says and punches him again. I can already tell that this relationship is going to involve a lot of fist-to-arm contact.

Helena and Vinny arrive. "Hello," Vinny greets us in his raspy voice, and then he does the what's-up nod to Anthony and Anthony does the what's-up nod back.

"You want anything to eat?" Anthony asks Bridget.

"Black licorice," Bridget says.

"Would you like anything?" Vinny asks Helena.

"Why don't you get whatever you want and I'll have some," Helena says.

"But I want to get something you want," Vinny tells her.

"Vinny, I don't know what I want, that's why I'm asking you to choose. Can you choose, please?"

"Okay," Vinny says.

"Don't worry, guys, I don't want anything," I add, and everyone laughs even though I wasn't trying to be funny.

Anthony and Vinny head over to the concession stand, and Helena steps toward Bridget and me conspiratorially. "I'm not sure I can truly love Vinny," she whispers.

"No!" Bridget says in mock surprise.

"He's such a sweetheart. He has such a kind soul," Helena says. "But I think I might need someone who's more assertive and less puppy dog." She looks genuinely sad and disappointed. Only some-one who sees such beauty in people could be so disappointed when she discovers it's not enough.

Somehow I end up sitting between the two couples. In spite of a possible breakup, Helena and Vinny hold hands for the entire movie, interlacing their fingers tightly, as if one of them might die if the other let go. Vinny nuzzles her neck and she keeps whispering for him to pay attention. On the other side of me, Bridget and Anthony keep kissing. And if that's not bad enough, toward the end of the movie I spot two familiar heads several rows in front of me, the über-blonde and the guy who likes her. I tell myself not to look, but I can't help it. There is Serena, massaging the back of Asher's neck with her hands. There is Serena, running her fingers through his hair. There is Serena, doing something to his ear—probably blowing a giant pink bubble into his ear canal. Maybe she'll make him go deaf and he'll stop liking her. Bridget and Anthony are now making out hard-core, like the only oxygen left on earth is in each other's mouths. I look down at my lap and start to wish. I wish I had no peripheral vision. I wish I was the one blowing a bubble in Asher's ear. I wish this movie was over.

In the lobby after the movie, I tell Vinny and Anthony that they're not allowed to walk out with us because I know my father will already be waiting outside.

"What would happen if I ran outside and started kissing you in front of your dad?" Anthony says.

For this he receives another punch in the arm from Bridget. "Nina's dad would *kill* her if you did that," she informs him.

"He wouldn't *kill* me," I protest. I must defend my father. He may be conservative, but he's no murderer like those nutty Islamic fanatics they show on TV movies who marry unsuspecting white women, then kidnap their daughters and take them to some unnamed Middle Eastern country. He wouldn't kill me, just yell and maybe cry and only ever let me out of the house for school.

A group of classmates gathers around us and everyone starts talking about going to the Greek diner for dessert. I want to leave before Asher and Serena show up so I say goodbye to my friends and take off. My father is at the end of the block. The car windows are halfway down and he's playing, what else, *qawwali* music and Nusrat Fateh Ali Khan's voice is drifting out into the street. A bunch of kids from my school are lingering on the sidewalk in front of the theater doors, talking loudly underneath a cloud of cigarette smoke. "Nice music!" a guy yells. He has his arms around Heather Esposito, who is wearing supertight acid-washed jeans and black boots with spurs on them.

I try not to make eye contact as I walk past. As soon as I get in the car I roll my window up and turn the music down. My father is gripping the steering wheel a little too hard. I can tell those kids make him nervous.

"Can you not play your music so loudly? Can't you play any other kind of music?" I ask.

"But I like this music," my father says. "Those young people over there are smoking. Your friends don't do that, do they?"

"Nope," I say. "No way." And this, at least, is the truth. My father starts to drive and I hold my breath and don't release it until we've reached the far end of Main Street, out of sight of the smoking young people.

Suicide Bride

The next day, Nasreen Khala comes to visit. *"As-salam alaikum,"* I say when I see her.

She nods approvingly. I bet she's thinking, at least my niece knows how to say *salaam* properly. Then she embraces me in what is supposed to be a hug but feels more like a death grip, my face flattened against her breast. She smells like she always does, a florid bouquet of fennel seeds, perfume, perspiration, and coconut oil. "Why did you cut your hair so short?" she says in Urdu after I am released.

My hand goes up to my hair, which reaches the top of my shoulders. After being forced to witness the Asher-Serena love affair grow from inception to adulthood, the last thing I need is a critique of my physical appearance. Luckily, my mother intervenes. "Let's unpack your suitcases," she says, and leads Nasreen Khala upstairs.

Nasreen Khala stays with us for a week, in the room across the hall from mine. This means I have to play my music really low and keep my door open most of the time, because my mother doesn't want Nasreen Khala to see my door closed and interpret it as some kind of physical and emotional barrier I put up between my parents and me, which of course is exactly what it is. Nasreen Khala brings me presents, two *shalwar kameez* and a choker made of black and gold beads that I have to admit is pretty cool-looking. She also brings an album containing photographs spanning the last few decades or so, and one day when I get home from school she and my mother are in the family room, looking at the photos.

"Look at this, Nina!" my mother exclaims. "My wedding."

It's a black-and-white photograph of my parents on their wedding day. They have a similar, color version of it framed in their bedroom, except in that one it's just the two of them. In this photo they're sitting on a sofa on a stage. My father is wearing something that looks like long streamers of red roses over his face that he's pushing aside with his hands so the camera can get a good shot of his big smile. My mother has a huge gold hoop through her nose and a *dupatta* over her head with a tasseled fringe on it. Her eyes are downcast. Unlike my father, my mother isn't smiling or even looking up in any of her wedding photographs, as it wasn't the custom for brides to do this back then. She looks like she could slit her wrists. I refer to it as the suicide-bride look, which my mother doesn't find very amusing. Sitting next to my mother is Nasreen Khala, at least fifty pounds lighter, wearing her hair in two long braids. About twenty people are crowded behind the sofa, trying to fit into the picture. I don't recognize any of them.

"Who are all of these people?" I ask.

"They're my cousins," my mother says, brushing her finger over their faces.

I look at the photograph again. On the sofa next to my father is an older woman with the same wide face and thin lips as my mother, but who has a much smaller frame. She is wearing a sari and sitting up very straight. "Who is that?" I ask.

"That's your nani," Nasreen Khala answers sharply. "You don't recognize her?"

Nani was my mother's mother. She died when I was five. I last saw her when I was a baby, so I have no memories of her.

"Of course she does. She didn't look carefully enough," my mother says.

I am certain Nasreen Khala wants to make some comment about me being umreecanized and disconnected from my extended family, but she holds her tongue. I look again. The woman in the picture resembles my mother, but I can't tell she's Nani. My version of Nani is the eight-by-ten photo hanging on our living room wall that shows her with rounded shoulders and white hair and deep wrinkles traversing her cheeks and neck.

"Guess what?" my mother tells me. "Nasreen Khala and I were talking, and I've decided that this December we're going to go to Pakistan."

"You say that every year," I respond.

"This time I mean it. If there are still tickets left, I'm going to book them," she says.

"Exciting, yes?" Nasreen Khala asks.

Exciting may not be the best word, but it's not so far off, either. It's about time I saw my parents' homeland, even though it'll probably mean meeting a million relatives I don't know and may never see again.

"I told your khalu you are coming to visit and he is thrilled," Nasreen Khala says. She's talking about her husband—Khalu is what you call your mother's sister's husband in Urdu. In Urdu, practically every relative has his or her own specific title. "He said he'll plan a trip to the ancient ruins of Moenjodaro."

I have a vague recollection of Khalu explaining to a young, fascinated Sonia how advanced the water and sanitation systems of this ancient city were for their time. "Sounds cool," I say, and it does, since I've never seen any ancient ruins.

At night we pray the *isha namaz*. My mother usually performs this prayer by herself. My father and I hardly ever pray, but whenever Nasreen Khala is here, we all pray together. Nasreen Khala's family always prays together at night, and she's very proud of this fact. Apparently the family that prays together stays together. I wonder if Nasreen Khala thinks that we pray like this when she isn't here, or if she's figured out that we do it only because my mother wants her to think that she is raising her children as properly as Nasreen Khala is, even though every time I open my mouth I quickly dispel this illusion.

My mother, Nasreen Khala, and I form a row and my father stands in front of us. He leads the prayer, reciting the Arabic suras quickly, often mumbling, not like the imam at the mosque in Albany who sings every word. As a Muslim, you're supposed to pray five times a day, but whenever I do pray, I don't feel very spiritual. To be honest, I feel a little bored. I repeat the prayers in Arabic and perform the motions, and my mind always wanders. I think about school, or my friends, or what movie I should rent next from the video store, or that the hair on my arms is growing back and I should wax them soon. I think about Asher and how I should not be thinking about Asher, and how starting tomorrow I will definitely not think about him. The only part of the prayer that gets my utmost attention is when you say your *du'a* at the end. You bend your head and cup your hands together and make requests of Allah. I ask for the same things, mostly. "Dear Allah. Please take care of my family and friends. Please let me get in to the college of my choice." I would ask Allah to make Asher dump Serena and fall for me, and then somehow change my parents' views on dating so that Asher and I could be boyfriend and girl-friend, but I prefer to keep my requests realistic. That way I have less chance of being disappointed.

The *B* Word

October 9 is almost here. The day of my birth. I'll be sixteen this year. The big one-six. I've never been into celebrating my birthday. I hate the attention, the singing, the cake, the good wishes, the expectations that this year will be better, brighter. When my parents were growing up in Pakistan they didn't celebrate their birthdays, but in spite of this my mother always feels bad that neither Sonia nor I ever want to celebrate ours. "But don't you want a party?" she used to ask. "All the kids have parties." After the age of eight, the only time Sonia allowed Ma to throw her a party was for her high school graduation, because she said she needed as much money as she could get to spend at college. My parents had it at the Deer Hook Country Club and invited their friends and Sonia made nearly three thousand dollars. Her cake said "Best of Luck at Harvard!" As if she needed it.

The first person to broach the *B* word is Helena. We have French together first period and we're in the lobby, waiting for the bell to ring. French is my least favorite class and having it so early in the morning makes it even worse. They've turned the heat on at school and Helena cracks open the window next to the trophy case to let the crisp fall air in. "I know you hate your birthday," Helena begins.

"I don't hate it, I just prefer not to celebrate it," I correct her.

"But it's your sixteenth and don't you think you should do something?" she continues.

"You didn't do anything for yours."

"Because of Paris," Helena reminds me. She asked her father to save the money he would have spent throwing her a party because she wants to go to Paris the summer after we graduate. For years, Helena has been dreaming of her big trip to Paris, the red-haired romantic running loose in the city of love. She's built it up so much in her head, I hope she's not disappointed when she gets there. "Well, at least ask your parents to get you something nice. You deserve it!" she says.

"Why, because I stayed alive long enough to turn sixteen?" I say. "Anyway, I don't know what I'd want except money. I don't wear diamond earrings or lingerie." On Helena's birthday, her mother mailed her a pair of diamond earrings and a purple lacy bra with matching underwear with a card that read, "Now that you are a grown woman, here are two things every grown woman should have—diamond solitaires and nice lingerie." The bra was an A cup, and Helena is a C, and she spent part of her birthday crying because her mother didn't know her bra size.

"There must be something," Helena insists.

"Well, I'd like to see Asher break up with bubble-gum head."

"I meant something that can come wrapped in a box. And anyway, I don't think that's going to happen anytime soon," she says, looking down the hall. I follow her gaze. Serena is whispering into, or perhaps sucking on, Asher's ear in front of the boys' bathroom. Every time I see them in such close proximity, an iron fist clenches my heart, then releases it suddenly, which must be what people mean when they say they're having heart pangs. Ask not for whom my heart pangs, it pangs for thee, Asher.

"Nina?" Helena waves her hand in my face. "Listen, you have to remember that there are so many other fish in the sea."

I shake my head. "Have you seen this sea?"

Helena's curled her hair into ringlets today and she wraps one around her finger. "Are you going to be as negative at sixteen as you are at fifteen?" she asks.

"No," I tell her. "I'll probably be more negative."

She gives me a kiss on the cheek. "Well, I'll still be your dearest friend." The bell rings. *"Allons-y!"* she says merrily, and I scowl at her.

The next person to bring up the *B* word is my mother. We're in the produce section of the grocery store. "Are you sure you don't want to invite your friends over for your birthday?" she asks.

"To do what, play musical chairs and eat cupcakes?" I snap. "I don't want to do anything."

"I could plan a party, invite some of your Pakistani friends, like Asiya and Saba, and their families. But I'd need some time to plan it."

"No parties," I tell her. "If you guys want to get me something, give me some money. I need to start saving for college."

"College," my mother says, staring down at a dented tomato. She puts her arm around me. "Nina, you are getting older, and life will become more complicated. You can talk to me about anything. It's good to talk to your mother because mothers always have your best interests in mind. Your mother is your real best friend."

Great. Next thing you know she'll be whipping out a sleeping bag and wanting to have a sleepover. You can talk to me about anything, she says. I doubt it's true, but I decide to test her claim. Maybe, for once, my mother will surprise me. Maybe we really can be friends. She puts some tomatoes in the cart and moves on to the eggplants. I follow her, contemplating what I should "confide."

"I have something to tell you," I say.

She looks surprised. She obviously didn't expect me to start confiding in her so soon. "Tell me."

"Remember that boy who called me last month?"

"The boy from the Volunteer Society," she says.

"I think he might like me."

My mother puts her finger to her lips and pulls me toward her until we're both huddled over the eggplants. "How do you know this? Did he tell you he likes you?"

I nod. I wonder how Robbie Nash would feel about how I'm using him in the "could I ever really be friends with my mother" litmus test.

"I knew it! That sneaky boy! The bake sale was only an excuse so he could call you. Don't worry, I will handle this." She makes a fist around an eggplant in her hand and shakes it like a maraca.

I've made a grave mistake. "Ma, have mercy on the eggplant."

She drops it in our cart. "Come," she says, and now I follow her to the salad dressings, where she picks up a bottle and holds it out in front of us like we're reading the label together. "You told him that you're Muslim and you don't date, right?"

"Yes."

"But did you tell him firmly?"

I nod again.

"Well," my mother continues, "if he keeps bothering you, you should quit the Volunteer Society. And if he still bothers you, I can call his mother."

"Don't worry," I say. "He already likes another girl."

"Which girl?"

"What do you care?" I say. "It's not me."

"These American boys, they want one thing," she says. "They have no respect for women."

"Some of them are very nice, Ma."

"Nina, don't be foolish. Of course they are nice, but first they will try and kiss you, and then they will try and do something else to you, and then they will get you pregnant. And then, then you will understand how nice they really are."

"Did you know there was phosphoric acid in salad dressing?" I ask.

My mother performs her deathly narrowing-eye, pressed-lips combo. "Be serious, Nina. Do you understand what I'm saying?"

"Don't worry, Ma. I told you he doesn't like me anymore."

The possibility that I might like the boy back hasn't even occurred to her. She just assumed that of course I wouldn't like him, because a good Pakistani Muslim girl would never like a boy until it was time for her to get married, to a good Pakistani boy, of course. In my mother's perception of high school, the relationships between boys and girls don't even have the potential for tenderness and emotional growth—there's no complexity in high school gender interactions, only extremes. The boys run around intent on taking the girls' virginity and the girls either snub them entirely or lie down in submission. They should have a Take Your Mother to High School Day so my mother could see what it's really like, though I bet you anything as soon as we got there we'd run right into Asher and Serena with their tongues down each other's throats, and my mother would clap her hands. "I told you so!" she'd say triumphantly as Asher and Serena made out behind her. But if she really was my best friend, she'd express her sympathy instead of triumph, because she'd be able to sense how upset the sight of those two makes me, and the awful pangings of my heart.

What's Your Score?

Every year Samina Auntie, one of my parents' friends, has a luncheon, and this year it falls on the same day as my birthday. I try to get out of going, but my mother makes the clucking sound she sometimes uses as a substitute for no. "Of course you have to go. Asiya always comes to our house when we have a party." Asiya is Samina Auntie's daughter. "And," my mother continues, "if you don't come, what will everyone say?"

The way my mother acts sometimes, you'd think What Everyone Will Say is the force that rules the universe. Pakistanis, at least the ones my parents know, do seem to have a lot to say about the activities of others in their community. The fact that the Prophet Muhammad frowned upon gossip and backbiting doesn't stop my mother or the other aunties from devoting a lot of their conversations to it. Gossip is one of their favorite pastimes.

Samina Auntie lives more than an hour away from us, in a two-story red brick house in a development full of other, identical two-story red brick houses. By the time we arrive, there's no parking left near Samina Auntie's house and my father drops us off in front so my mother won't have to walk far in her heels. Like her nail polish, my mother has at least a hundred pairs of heels to go with her outfits. She buys them at discount shoe stores when they have clearance sales and owns every imaginable shade of green, red, pink, brown, yellow, and so on and so forth. Today she's wearing a light pink *shalwar kameez* with matching light pink nail polish and shoes. I'm also in a *shalwar kameez*. The material is kind of stiff and poofs out at the waist and makes me look like a member of the Future Fairy Godmothers of America Club.

As we enter my mother whispers for me to say *salaam* to all of the aunties. "I know," I hiss. This habit of my mother's is a pet peeve of mine. Even though I've been to a million of these parties, she always has to remind me of the proper way to greet the aunties, as if one time I might forget and walk around the party asking the aunties "What's hanging?" instead of politely saying *salaam*.

The aunties are gathered in the kitchen, drinking soda out of red and blue plastic cups, so I can hit them all at once. *"As-salam alaikum,"* I say.

Samina Auntie comes right at me. When I was young I was convinced she was a witch because of the giant mole on her left cheek with its one black hair that curls out from the center. "Nina! How are you, *beti*?" Samina Auntie is a chin pincher. Her hand reaches for my face and before I can move she makes contact, squeezing my chin between her thumb and forefinger.

"I'm fine."

"You've put on a little weight since I last saw you," she says. I choose to neither confirm nor deny this. "When are you going to Harvard?"

"I just started my junior year of high school."

My mother smooths down my hair with her hand. "Nina will go to Yale," she declares. "One daughter at Harvard, one at Yale." If my parents had a theme song, this would be the chorus.

The aunties resume their conversations and I head down to the basement. The little kids are on the floor in front of the television playing video games, and I know the older girls will be hanging out in Asiya's bedroom in the back of the basement, so I knock on the door.

"Who is it?" someone calls out from inside.

"It's me, Nina."

Asiya opens the door. I see her and the other girls here, Saba and Huma, once a month or so, at various Pakistani events and parties and at the mosque for Eid prayers.

"We're trying to keep the boys out," Asiya says. Asiya is older than me, a freshman at one of the local colleges. She has light brown highlights and her hair is always shiny like someone just polished it. She's wearing gold eye shadow. My mother claims Asiya is too concerned with her looks and not enough with studying, which she thinks is especially disappointing considering her mother is a successful doctor. Apparently Samina Auntie told Asiya that if she's not interested in a career, she might as well get married, and has started looking for a suitable boy for her. "How are things in that little town of yours?"

All of these girls live in or close to Albany. To them, Deer Hook is the boondocks. "They're fine," I say, having a seat on the floor, next to Saba. Huma is sitting opposite me. I haven't seen her in a while.

She's older than all of us, a senior in college. She and my sister used to be friends when they were young.

"How's your sister?" Huma asks. "I haven't seen her in years."

That makes two of us. "She's good, studying hard at Harvard," I say.

"Harvard." Huma shakes her head. "I still remember her teaching me the multiplication tables when she was five."

"Sounds like Sonia," I say.

"Well, tell her I said hi." Huma looks down and starts playing with the hem of her *kameez*. Everyone is silent and fidgety and it feels like there's something heavy hanging in the air, the weight of which has sealed everyone's lips.

"Did I interrupt something?" I ask. I hope they say no—I don't want to have to offer to leave and hang out with the young kids or in the kitchen full of aunties or in the living room full of uncles watching a videotape of the Cricket World Cup final.

"Huma's boyfriend asked her to marry him," Asiya says, and Huma flashes her a look. "Don't worry, Nina's cool," Asiya insists. "Right, Nina?" I nod, a little too eagerly.

"Please don't tell anyone," Huma pleads, looking at me with her large, doe-y eyes.

"Maybe you should tell your mother," Saba says.

"I won't tell her unless I decide to marry him." Huma folds her legs in front of her, mermaid-style. She has a long, thin neck and a narrow face, and that combined with those bedroom eyes give her an air of fragility. If we were on a sinking ship she'd definitely be the first to be rescued.

"Ian is a sweetheart," Asiya says. "You love him and he loves you and you guys have to get married." Asiya and Huma attend the same college, which is how she must know Huma's boyfriend.

"I do love Ian," Huma responds. "But I just don't know if I can do it." So my sister's old playmate is now in love.

Asiya nods. "That's why I've been turning down every guy that's been asking me out. I mean, I go on a date with one of these guys, and then we go on another, and then we fall in love, and then what?"

"And then this," Huma responds. She sighs and tilts her head, offering us a lovely view of the elegant curve of her neck. I wonder if Ian has kissed this particular curve. If he hasn't yet, he should soon because it sounds like their future is uncertain.

"At least boys ask you out," Saba says. "In my school, I'm like the Paki pariah."

I raise my hand. "Make that two of us."

"Oh, I was too, in high school," Asiya says. This is total bull and we all know it. Asiya's awkward phase lasted about two seconds. "Sometimes high school boys are too stupid and immature to appreciate you. Wait until college, you'll be pushing them away."

The idea of me ever having to push boys away is comical, to say the least. Saba must agree because she rolls her eyes at me.

"Let's talk about something other than boys," Huma says.

"My aunt came from Pakistan and brought me these bangles." Asiya displays them for us. The bangles are delicate and intricate, but I'm paying more attention to her arms, which are blissfully smooth. She must notice me looking, because she says, "I just waxed." She sighs. "I wish they always would stay this way."

It's too bad I'm not an actual fairy godmother, because then I could grant her wish. "Tell me about it," I say. As much as I complain about having to go to Pakistani parties, it is nice to be in a safe space where you can talk about waxing and body hair and not feel like a freak.

"Oh, please. My arms are the absolute worst," Saba announces, pushing up her sleeves so we can see. It's like the hairy girls' show-and-tell hour. Personally, I think mine are the absolute worst. Saba's skin is the color of dark chocolate and the black hair isn't as apparent as it is on mine, but I'm too embarrassed to offer up my own arms as a contestant.

"Keep waxing them. The more you wax, the less hair grows back over time," Asiya tells us, adjusting her *dupatta* until the gold embroidered edges are facing the right way.

"Is that why you're always waxing your upper lip?" Zeeshan, Asiya's older brother, has stuck his head in the doorway. He is the male version of Asiya, tall and cute with a wide smile and broad shoulders. There are not that many attractive Pakistani boys in our community and you can tell Zeeshan is used to being admired. He's attending a six-year medical program and I'm surprised he's even here, since usually when boys start college their attendance at these parties begins to dwindle. Zeeshan's esteem among the aunties and uncles has reached its highest level yet. Pretty soon a lot of the aunties will be clamoring for him to marry their daughters. Whenever he enters my vicinity at a party I always get a little flutter in my stomach. There is something very disarming about his smile.

"Don't you know how to knock?" Asiya snaps.

"I'm going out to get some pizza," he says. "You guys want anything?"

Asiya shakes her head and Zeeshan leaves. "My mother would

never let me leave like that in the middle of a party. It's so unfair; she lets Zeeshan do practically whatever he wants. He even got to go to prom with his friends." She takes some pink-tinted lip balm out of her purse and dabs it on her lips before continuing. "And even though we're both going to local colleges, he's allowed to live in the dorms. She will never let me live in the dorms!"

"Of course she won't," Huma comments. "You're a girl and he's a boy and there's a double standard that must be followed."

"Well, it's different, you know," I say. The girls turn toward me, curious. I put on my best auntie voice. "Boys can't get pregnant."

After a second of silence, we start laughing. For a minute, the chains that bind us bond us, and we are grateful for one another. Then Yasmin Auntie, Huma's mother, knocks on the door and enters without waiting for a response. I look at the floor, worried that somehow she might be able to read her daughter's secret on my face. "Nina," she says. "How is your sister?"

"She's good, thanks," I say.

Yasmin Auntie nods. She's very different from Huma, a thick woman with small eyes and a commanding voice. "Lunch is ready," she informs us, and we follow her upstairs.

"Girls!" my mother says as we walk into the kitchen. "Why were you hiding in the basement?"

"Oh, we were just catching up, Farzana Auntie," Asiya replies.

"Why don't you ever catch up with us?" Samina Auntie asks, and her hand reaches out, aiming for Saba, whose chin is the closest.

"They think we are boring," my mother says, and the three of them titter. "Nina, look at how nicely Asiya matched her jewelry to her clothes. You should learn from her."

"You are too skinny," Samina Auntie tells Huma. "Boys want to marry girls who are slim, not skinny. Come, eat!"

The dining room is lined with platters of food: Hyderabadi *biryani* with saffron and mint and egg curry and kababs and lentils and chutneys and naan. Every year Samina Auntie's luncheon is exactly the same as the last, except people are a little taller or a little fatter or a little balder, like my father, who is heading our way, the top of his head as shiny as the silverware, a plate full of food in his hands. "Chow time!" he says to us as he walks by, and he looks so happy and excited I have to smile.

We sit down in the corner of the living room with the aunties and eat quietly, listening to their conversation. My mother is talking to Samina Auntie and another one of her friends, Nilofer Auntie. Ever since I've known her, Nilofer Auntie has been in a state of perpetual displeasure. She usually has a frown on her face and always shifts uncomfortably in her seat like she's trying to dislodge a wedgie. But she must derive some pleasure from the act of gossip because she's often engaging in it, like now. She's talking about a wedding she went to.

"But the boy converted," Samina Auntie says.

"All you have to do to convert is say the *shahadah*," Nilofer Auntie disagrees. "I am sure he is Muslim by name only. It looked so funny, a Pakistani girl wearing a traditional red bridal *gharara* and a white boy in a white suit. He was not even that good-looking. And the people on the boy's side were going to the hotel bar and buying drinks. Even the groom's mother was drinking! By the end of the reception, she was drunk. Her cheeks were red and she kept laughing loudly." Nilofer Auntie is swaying her head, imitating the drunk woman laughing. "Hee-haw hee-haw!" I don't know why she thinks drunk people laugh like donkeys.

"Well, this is the risk we take by raising our children in America," Huma's mother says. "If we're not careful, in three generations, they won't even look Pakistani, let alone speak Urdu."

I can't help but cast a sideways glance at Huma, whose head is bent over her plate, her hair falling so far forward you can't see her face.

After we eat, Samina Auntie tells everyone to reassemble in the dining room for dessert. "Especially you girls," she says, and waits for us to get up. As we walk into the dining room everyone parts, making a path for us so we can stand right at the center of the table, as if the desserts have been displayed in our honor. "She's here," my mother calls out, and in walks Samina Auntie with a huge birthday cake lit up with candles. The adults start clapping their hands and singing "Happy birthday, dear Nina," and the little kids start singing "You look like a monkey" and giggling, and then everyone is saying "Make a wish! Make a wish!"

Birthday wishes are so hard because you have to make them under a time constraint and you get only one. I close my eyes. *Please make Asher like me.* But when I open my eyes to blow out the candles, they're already being blown out by Samina Auntie's youngest son, who has somehow maneuvered his way in front of me. "Ahmad!" Samina Auntie cries as he blows out the last candle. She runs over and drags him away by his wrist.

"Pretend to blow them out," someone suggests.

"No, no, I'll light them again," Samina Auntie calls out.

"It's okay," I say. Sometimes it's better to let a moment go rather than try to capture it again. I pick up the knife and cut the cake. My father is taking pictures so I try to look as happy as I can considering that little twerp just stole my birthday wish. There's more clapping and now everyone wants to congratulate me, like I've accomplished something extraordinary by turning sixteen.

"Little Nina has become big Nina!" Samina Auntie says, squeezing my chin. "So sorry about my naughty son. You know how boys can be!"

"Nina, you know, I already have a nice boy in mind for you. I'm waiting for your mother to give me the word," Uzma Auntie, Saba's mother, tells me.

"Let her start college first," my mother says.

And here I am, at the center of attention, exactly where I didn't want to be. The aunties and uncles form a receiving line and congratulate me one by one and ask me about my future: where am I going to college, which career path am I going to follow? I offer the appropriate answers: Yale, and maybe medicine. My mother stands next to me nodding. She looks so proud, I would never dare answer their questions truthfully—that I have no idea where I'm going to go to college or what I want to do with my life.

Farid Uncle and his wife are the last ones left. Farid Uncle, who, for as long as I have known him, has had a large mustache that curls up at the ends like a villain from a Bollywood film, tousles my hair. "*Beta*, remember us when you go to Harvard!" he says.

"Yale," my mother corrects him.

Mumtaz Auntie, his wife, who dyes her hair a light shade of brown and has bright green eyes, courtesy of colored contacts, asks, "Will you get a perfect score on the SATs, like your sister?"

Sonia didn't get a perfect score, but I don't bother correcting her. "We'll see."

"You know, Salman has started his third year at Dartmouth. We were just visiting him in New Hampshire last weekend," Mumtaz Auntie says, pronouncing it New Hamp-shy-er, as though hobbits live there.

"And he is vice president of the Muslim Student Association," Farid Uncle adds. I've talked to Salman only once or twice, years ago. He was a skinny, quiet kid who was obsessed with Hercule Poirot mysteries and once asked me if I thought he had an egg-shaped head. All of the adults speak very highly of him. Salman scores big on the Pakistani second-generation prestige scale, at least in our parents' eyes.

It's as though there's an unofficial Pakistani prestige point system; the higher your score, the more esteem you hold among the aunties and uncles, and the more attractive you are as a marriage prospect for their sons and daughters. Everyone starts out with zero, and points are added and subtracted based on different types of criteria. For example:

+5 if you're a doctor

+4 if you went to an Ivy League school

+3 if you're a businessman, a lawyer (the moneymaking kind), or an engineer

+2 if you're fair, if you speak Urdu, or if you're moderately religious

+1 if you're slim (for a woman), or if you're tall (for a man)

-1 if you can't speak Urdu, or if you're fat or short

-2 if you can't understand Urdu, or if you're dark

-3 if you're a religious fanatic

-4 if you're an artist, musician, poet, or anything else in the creative fields

-5 if you're gay or an atheist

Salman has to be at least an eleven. So does Sonia. Asiya's brother Zeeshan is up there too. If I do get into an Ivy League school, I'll be at least a six. But I have a feeling, when everything is said and done, that my score could end up in the negatives, and so I will be a disappointment to my parents, and the aunties and uncles will be reluctant to allow their sons to marry me. But, once you're able to leave home, maybe the amount of fun you have is inversely proportional to your prestige score, which would mean all those gay Pakistani atheists out there must be having the absolute time of their lives.

And the Devil Makes Three

During the car ride home, my mother summarizes Nilofer Auntie's comments about the wedding she attended. My father shakes his head and makes disapproving sounds in his throat at the appropriate moments.

"Sometimes I wonder if we did the right thing in coming here," my mother says. "In Pakistan, at least you know your daughters will marry Muslims."

"You shouldn't worry. We raised our daughters well. I have full faith in them," my father says. I don't understand why my father has so much faith in me. But I suppose I've never done anything to make him think otherwise.

My mother turns around, arms folded. "Nina, remember that you should never be alone with a boy, ever. Because when a boy and a girl are alone together, there is always a third person with them. Do you know who that third person is?"

"Shaitaan," I answer. I have heard this one, like, a zillion times. You would think the devil has better things to do than hang out with adolescents. I picture a teenage couple at the movies with the devil sitting in between them, trying to eat popcorn with his hooves, his two horns casting a shadow on the movie screen, and start to giggle.

"Why are you laughing?" my mother asks, frowning. She'll never find any humor in this topic.

"Oh, just something Asiya said," I tell her, and she doesn't press further.

"Nina, I forgot to tell you," she says. "I bought our tickets to Pakistan. Your father and I are going a few days before you and Sonia because you need to finish your semesters. But do you think you two will be okay, flying all the way to Pakistan by yourselves?" She looks at me, her face tense with worry.

"Of course," I tell her. "All we have to do is get on a plane and get off it, right?"

"They'll be fine, Farzana," my father says.

"I'll never forget my first time on a plane," she says. "I was flying to New York to join your father. I was sitting by the window and I was so scared I kept my eyes closed during takeoff and landing. I had a *suparah* from the Quran in my purse, which I hugged to my chest for most of the flight, and I think the man next to me thought I was doing this because I was worried he'd steal it. Anyway, I'll give you and Sonia those gold lockets I have with the Ayat al-Kursi inside. Make sure you wear them on the plane."

The Ayat al-Kursi is a verse from the Quran that Muslims recite or wear or carry with them because it is supposed to help protect you from evil. I know it by heart and I can read it. When I was in sixth grade, my mother hired a man from the Albany mosque named Brother Hassan to come to our house once a week to teach me to read the Quran. Muslims are supposed to learn how to read the Quran, even though most of us can't understand the classical Arabic it's written in. Brother Hassan arrived on a Saturday. I chose my favorite headscarf, light pink with beaded embroidery on the edges, and tied it onto my head before going downstairs. When I looked in the mirror I could hardly recognize myself. With the scarf on, I seemed like such a sweet girl, not a girl who snuck teen romance novels home from school in her backpack. Brother Hassan and I sat at the table in the sunroom. The man who taught Quran lessons to Sonia, Brother Musa, was so old and hard of hearing that Sonia had to yell into his ear when she read. But Brother Hassan was young, in his thirties, and had blue eyes and a short, trimmed beard. We went through the Arabic alphabet: *alif, baa, taa,* ... By the end of the second hour I had succeeded in reciting the alphabet by heart. Brother Hassan smiled at me, his blue eyes shining. "Mashaallah, you are very smart," he said. I smiled back.

Then, at the end of the lesson, Brother Hassan pointed at a painting on the wall. It was of two Mexican women in a field, holding bright red and yellow flowers in their hands. My mother loved it and even grew red and yellow flowers in pots that she brought into our sunroom every winter and positioned right underneath, though they were never as vivid as the ones in the painting. "Tell your mother to take that painting down," he said. "It is *haram* to depict human figures."

When I told my mother this, she said, "What?" so I repeated it. She put her hands on her head and stroked her straight black hair, smoothing it against her scalp. My mother always had to flatten her hair before she thought hard about something. Finally she said, "What can you do?"

Brother Hassan never returned. I still had to learn how to read the Quran and my mother spent the next ten Saturdays teaching me herself, under the watchful eyes of the Mexican women.

Stone of Love

All of that time spent talking to the aunties and uncles has exhausted me and I take a nap as soon as we get home, only to be rudely awakened by my mother.

"Let me sleep," I beg.

"You've slept for over an hour," she says. "You need to get up and get dressed."

"Why? I'm not going anywhere." I lie on my stomach and pull the covers over my head. "It's my birthday and I don't have to get up."

"Fine," my mother says.

"Too lazy to get out of bed, you big bum?"

I flip over, startled. Bridget and Helena are standing over me. My mother is behind them, laughing.

"Surprise!" Bridget cries out.

"Happy birthday!" Helena says.

"What are you guys doing here?"

Helena sits down on my bed. "If Nina won't go to the mountain, the mountain will come to Nina."

"Ma, you knew about this?" I ask.

"Maybe, maybe not," she says, which of course means that she did. "Come downstairs for food when you're ready."

After my mother leaves, Helena hands me a small box with a bow made of thick silver ribbon that I know she must have spent a long time trying to tie just right. "Your present."

"It's from both of us," Bridget says.

I open it. Inside is a gift certificate to Sleepy Hollow Books, the bookstore at the closest mall, and a pair of earrings, two dark-pink round stones dangling from silver wire. "They're beautiful," I say.

"They're rose quartz," Helena explains. "Rose quartz is the stone of love and healing. It's supposed to help you learn to love your true self and help others fall in love with you. My mother used to have a necklace made of it."

"Yeah, and she got divorced," Bridget says, winking at me.

"True, but it can't hurt, can it?" Helena insists.

"It certainly can't," I agree, putting them on.

"Now, get out of bed, birthday girl!" Bridget says. "My chutney is waiting."

"Let me use the bathroom first," Helena says, and as Bridget goes through my closet to see if there's anything she wants to borrow, I remember the first time they slept over, in fourth grade. We had convened in my bedroom and Bridget went to the bathroom, and when she came out she asked, "Why do you have a watering can in the bathroom?" She was talking about the light green plastic watering can with a round base that was tucked in between the toilet and the wall that I had forgotten to hide. I couldn't think of some believable lie as to why it would be there, so I told the truth instead.

"It's called a *lota*. Muslims use it to wash after going to the bathroom."

"Do they not have toilet paper in Pakistan?" Bridget asked. She didn't say it rudely, but I still felt ashamed and was too embarrassed to explain that the reason for the *lota* was not that we didn't have toilet paper, but that we considered washing to be more hygienic.

"Oh, it's just like the French. They use bidets," Helena said. I didn't know what a bidet was, but it sounded a lot more refined than my green plastic *lota*.

"Cool," Bridget said, shrugging, and, to my relief, neither of them ever brought it up again.

By the time we head downstairs, my mother has set out an impressive display of various snacks: samosas, *chaat*, fried *pakoras*, *chapli* kabobs. My father is sitting at the table, visually consuming the array of food before him, and he grins when he sees us because it means he's now allowed to actually eat.

"Hi, Dr. Khan," Helena says. "My dad wanted me to tell you hello."

"How is he doing?" my father asks. A few years ago, my father did a double bypass surgery on Helena's father.

"He's good. He says he hopes he never has to see you again."

My father laughs. "Tell him I hope so too."

"This is my chutney, right?" Bridget asks, pointing to the bowl of homemade tamarind chutney on the table. Whenever Bridget comes to our house my mother makes extra for her.

"It is. It's called *meethi* chutney," my mother says.

"*Meethi* chutney," Bridget repeats, and my mother smiles at me. She's told Bridget the name of it a bunch of times, but Bridget never remembers. "I love it."

"You can take some home if you want," my mother offers.

Bridget shakes her head. "I could never—that would be too much of a good thing." She keeps spooning the chutney into her bowl and soon her samosa looks like it's sitting in a brown soup.

Helena picks up a cauliflower *pakora*. "I love these. They're like the Pakistani version of tempura."

"Have it with the chutney," Bridget says, pushing the bowl toward her.

"Were you surprised, Nina?" my father asks.

I nod. "Very. Look at the earrings they gave me." I pull my hair back so my parents can admire them properly.

"Very pretty," my mother says. "I have shoes the same exact color."

"It's rose quartz," Helena pipes up. "It's the stone of lo—"

She stops midsentence because I flash her a warning look. The last thing I need is my parents questioning me later on why my friends think I need a stone that promotes love.

"The stone of what?" my mother asks.

"It's the stone of longevity," Bridget cuts in.

"I don't give it to my patients," my father jokes. "They wouldn't need me anymore!" Bridget and Helena laugh and he laughs too, happy to have such a receptive audience.

"I forgot how much I love that painting," Helena says, pointing to the painting of the three Mexican women. "It's very romantic."

"You know, I found it at a garage sale," my mother tells her. "Sometimes, when I look at it, I wish I could go to a place like that, where the colors of the flowers are so bright."

Helena nods appreciatively.

"You and Dad should go to Mexico," I say. "See those colors in real life."

"Yes, but it wouldn't be quite the same," my mother says.

Helena sighs. "It never is, is it?"

Bridget has finished almost the entire bowl of chutney. "You're such a great cook, Mrs. Khan. The only thing my mother can make well is brisket."

"Thank you, Bridget," my mother says. "I wanted to tell you girls that you should sign up for the same SAT prep course Nina is taking. It starts in January."

Helena and Bridget grimace at the mention of the test.

"It's pronounced S-A-T, Ma, not *sat*," I correct her.

"I hate standardized tests," Helena complains. "I don't do well under time pressure."

"That's why you should take this class. Sonia took it and it helped her a lot. They give practice tests to help you become accustomed to the time constraint." My mother sounds like a brochure for the prep center.

"Ma, my friends are here to relax, not get stressed out about an exam that's months away."

"Nina hates to talk about academics," my mother says. "Sonia used to discuss these things with me all the time. You girls know this year is the most important year for getting into college."

Helena and Bridget nod and I decide it's time to save them from further lectures. "What's the plan?" I ask.

"We thought we'd go to the diner for dessert," Helena says.

"It's not a birthday until the birthday girl eats cake," Bridget adds.

I glance at my mother, hoping she won't use the fact that I already had cake as an excuse not to let me go.

She looks at her watch. "Be back by ten," she says.

Bridget's mom's car smells like Opium perfume and cigarette smoke. We blast pop songs and sing along at the top of our lungs. Bridget and I are hopelessly off-key; we were both rejected from chorus in seventh grade. Helena, on the other hand, even had a solo in chorus once and sounds like a female maestro compared to us.

Bridget's still belting out the tunes as we enter the diner. " 'And I would walk five hundred miles . . .' "

"I would walk five hundred miles to get away from you right now," I tell her. We all laugh, not because it's funny but because it's Saturday night and it's my birthday and the three of us are together and about to eat something decadent. On top of everything else, I am sixteen, which sounds infinitely more grown up than fifteen, and Helena was right, it is a cause for celebration.

"Look," Bridget says. "There's Serena."

And there she is, at the other end of the diner, waving at us. And there, at the same table, sitting not across from her but right next to her, is Asher.

"We should go over and say hello," Helena says.

I shake my head. "This is just my luck."

"We'll say hi quickly and go sit down somewhere else," Helena reassures me.

"Fancy running into you three here," Serena says. The mayor of Deer Hook should issue a decree—people who begin sentences with the word *fancy* shall be chased out of town immediately. There's a plate of half-eaten banana cream pie in front of them and one of Asher's arms is resting along the top of the booth. Serena's head fits a little too neatly into the space under his shoulder and I don't feel like celebrating anymore.

"It's Nina's birthday," Bridget informs them, and Asher and Serena both smile up at me. "We're going to oink out on some dessert."

"Happy birthday, Nina!" Asher says. "Why don't you guys sit down? Dessert's on us."

I know he's looking at me, but I can't lift my eyes from the yellow table, and my cheeks are so flaming hot the cook could come out and broil some burgers on them.

"But we just paid the bill," Serena protests.

"We can still order more," Asher says.

"Thanks for the offer, Asher," Helena tells him. "But tonight is a girls' night out—no boys allowed."

Serena leans against Asher's chest. "Did you hear that, honey?" she purrs. "These girls don't want to hang out with you. Guess it's you and me for the rest of the night."

Asher doesn't respond and she starts petting his face as if he's some kind of cat, and maybe I'm wrong, but I swear that it's his cheeks that are now turning a little red.

"Nina?" Serena says. "Do you want some of our banana cream pie? There's no way we'll finish it."

Asher gently removes Serena's hand from his face and clasps it in his. "Don't you think the birthday girl deserves her own dessert?"

"Of course!" Serena exclaims. "I just thought she could have some of ours too, if she wanted." As if I would ever touch the dessert that those two had shared together. You might as well gargle the arrow that shattered your heart.

"I'll have some." Bridget picks up Serena's fork and digs in. "Yum," she says. "Delicious."

Serena turns to Asher. "We should go, right, honey? Let these girls have their girl time." She says this condescendingly, as if girl time is something that comes right before nap time in kindergarten.

Asher looks at his watch and nods. The couple rises, Serena clinging to Asher's side. "Happy birthday, Nina," Asher says again.

"Yes, happy birthday." Serena says this so sweetly I want to kill her. "Those are really pretty earrings."

"Thanks," I mumble. After they leave I snatch the fork out of Bridget's hand. "Can you not eat their stupid dessert?"

"What? It's good," Bridget says.

"Forget about them and their dessert," Helena tells me. "It's your birthday! You're not allowed to be sad!"

We get our own table and I order a hot fudge sundae, no cherry and lots of whipped cream. Though the chocolate helps some, it can't erase the image I have of Asher and Serena tucked into a booth together, sharing dessert and kissing and laughing. It can't mute the *keera* in my brain, who asks me, "Why can't that be you?" and it can't silence the depressing background music in my head, which has now changed from silly pop songs to a requiem for a love I never had.

The Fool in the Corner

I t's midterm week and I'm happy, for various reasons. All the studying is keeping me from thinking too much about Asher, and it's my favorite time of year in Deer Hook, when the leaves are at their most brilliant, and the palette of this normally dull town is transformed into intense reds and vibrant oranges.

Ms. Tazinski dismisses us from English class early, which is perfect because it gives me some time to cram for my math midterm. I've found a nice, quiet spot in the back of the library when Bridget materializes in front of me.

She puts her hand over my notebook. "Guess what."

"Just tell me."

"First guess."

"I don't want to guess, Bridget. I feel like I've been guessing at things all week."

"Whatever, like you ever have to guess at exams."

"Can you just tell me? And can you not talk so loudly? This is a library."

"Oh, fine." She lowers her voice to a whisper. "Asher and Serena had a big fight."

"About what?"

"I only talked to Serena for a few minutes last night, so I don't know the details, but something about Serena being too possessive," Bridget says. "So maybe there's hope for you!"

"What hope? Even if they do break up it doesn't mean he'll start liking me. 'Oh, my God, Nina, I can't believe I didn't like you before—I guess it was hard to see you behind Serena's boobs.'"

Bridget laughs. "Anyway, it's better than them being together, right? Anthony and I are going for Chinese after last period. You want to come? I'll drop you back home."

"Can't," I say. "I have to study for bio tonight."

Bridget sticks out her tongue. "And you call your sister a super-nerd."

I only manage to do one more problem before the bell rings. As I walk to precalc, I see Asher coming from the opposite direction, and purposely slow my pace so we'll reach the classroom at the same time.

"Hey, Nina," Asher says. There's dark stubble on his chin and the lower half of his cheeks, and the skin under his eyes is a little gray. "You ready for this?"

I've been studying hard and can't be more ready than I am, but I feign consternation. "No way. You?"

He shakes his head. "This is my toughest subject. I feel like I haven't slept in days, and when I do I have nightmares about math. Last night, I dreamed sine and cosine were these evil albino twins who kidnapped me and shaved my head. When I woke up I was so happy I still had hair." He runs his fingers through his messy waves and looks sheepish. "I must sound a little crazy."

"No, not at all," I say. Asher is not only speaking to me, he's speaking to me in contiguous sentences, and I never want it to end, but Mr. Porcupine is heading down the hall with a stack of exams in his arms.

"Well, good luck," Asher says. "Not that you'll need it."

After Mr. Porcupine passes out the exams it takes me a few minutes to focus. I can't believe that Asher and I had a proper conversation, and not only that, but there was something almost confessional about his dialogue—he wouldn't have told any random girl about his nightmares, right?

When the class ends, Asher is still scribbling in his test book. After I hand in my exam, I linger in the lobby of the school, pretending to read the announcements posted on the extracurriculars board as I plot the continuance of our conversation. I'll ask him how the exam went, and then I'll make a joke about the sine and cosine twins—but what joke? I can't be funny under pressure. Maybe it's better if I forgo humor and instead ask him things like which midterms he has left, and if it's true he loves to play basketball.

"Nina!" Helena is running across the lobby. When she reaches me she leans against the board, panting like she just ran two miles instead of thirty feet. "How was your test?" she gasps.

"It was fine. What is wrong with you?"

"What makes you think something's wrong?"

"Your eyes are only this bright when you're upset."

"Oh, Nina," she says. "I'm not going to New Mexico."

It takes me a second to figure out she's talking about Christmas vacation. Under the custody arrangement, Helena is supposed to spend a week over Christmas and a few weeks over the summer with her mother, who picks up and moves every few years, but is currently living in Santa Fe.

"She and her twenty-seven-year-old Austrian sculptor boyfriend are going to Austria for the holidays," Helena says. "And I'm supposed to go with them."

"But that sounds great."

"Oh, please. I've told you how my mother is whenever she starts a new relationship. I wanted my Christmas break to be quality time with my mother, not watching her make out in the Alps with her new boyfriend who's closer to my age than hers."

"Maybe it won't be so bad," I offer. It's strange to think of Helena having to watch her mother make out with someone. I rarely see my parents kiss, and when they do it's a chaste peck on the lips. In our culture, romantic displays of affection are supposed to remain behind closed doors.

"Maybe, but why can't it ever be just her and me?" she asks. I can't answer this and hug her instead. There's the sound of voices coming down the hallway. Asher is one of the first people to step into the lobby, looking even more tired than before. I wonder how he feels about the exam, and I want to approach him, but then I see Serena. She waves at him and he stops and she scurries over and they exchange a few words and then he leans down and kisses her on the lips. And so they've made up, and so they continue, through the lobby and down the hall at the other end, hand in hand. And so I am the fool in the corner, clinging to birthday wishes that will never come true.

Helena tosses her head, her aqua eyes still shining fiercely. "It's really not that bad, right? I mean, I get to be with my mother and I get to see Austria, right? It's not worth being upset over."

I glance over my shoulder in the direction Serena and Asher went, but they've disappeared from view. Neither is he, I tell myself. Neither is he.

Schwa-mergency

It takes a little more than a month of dating Anthony for Bridget to start turning into the mushy sentimentalist she swore she'd never be. "Anthony is awesome," she says to us at lunch one day. "I am totally falling in love."

"What have you done with Bridget?" I ask.

Bridget sighs. "I know. It's crazy. If you had told me last summer I was going to turn into one of those girls who can't shut up about her boyfriend, I would have told you that you must have been dropped on your head as a baby."

"I've lost both my friends to love," I say. "It was nice while it lasted."

Helena links arms with me. "You'll always have us. Anyway, I have to break up with Vinny sometime soon."

"For Chrissake, Helena," Bridget cries. "You've been telling us this for ages. Can you break up with him already?"

"It's not that simple," Helena protests. "He comes from a broken home."

"So do you," Bridget points out.

"I do not. I mean, I do, but it's not the same. Vinny's father took off when he was two, never calls or sends them any money, and his mother drinks too much, and she and his older brother are always getting into awful fights. They make my family look like the Cleavers."

"But you can't stay with someone because you feel sorry for him," I say.

"Do us all a favor—slap a Band-Aid on that bleeding heart," Bridget says.

Helena turns to her. "What happened to the 'Oh, isn't love grand' Bridget?"

"Just because I'm in love doesn't mean I'm going to be a sucker for it," she retorts.

"Amen," I say. Bridget raises her orange juice carton and I raise my water bottle and we toast.

"Hello, ladies," Anthony greets us. "What are you two toasting?"

Bridget beams at him. "Muscle man! I was just talking about you."

He sits down next to her. Bridget leans over to hug him and spills some of her juice onto his lap and Helena hands him napkins. She usually has extra, and Bridget never has enough. "Has she always been this clumsy?" he asks.

Helena laughs. "Always. Remember that time in sixth grade when she dropped her trombone on Mr. Lillis's foot and he had to go to the hospital?"

"That was Bridget? I remember our whole class running to the window so we could watch the ambulance."

"Can't help it, I'm a Sagittarian," Bridget says. "But wait till you see me on skis, Anthony. You won't even believe it's me, that's how unclumsy I am." She nudges him. "I am going to teach you how to ski this winter."

Anthony raises his index finger. "Sorry. I'm an island boy. I'm not getting on skis." Anthony's parents are from Grenada, which, according to him, is one of the most beautiful islands in the world.

SHEBA KARIM

"Oh, come on," Bridget says. "It'll be the sweetest thing you've ever done."

Anthony turns to her. "Oh, and how do you know all of the sweet things I've ever done?"

I sense Bridget is about to make a lewd comment, so I cut her off. "All right, happy couple, enough."

Bridget punches him. "We are a happy couple, aren't we, Anthony?"

"The happiest," he replies, kissing her on the cheek.

"You two are simply adorable," Helena says. I have to admit, they are pretty adorable. Would Asher laugh at my dumb jokes like Anthony laughs at Bridget's? Like my mother laughs at my father's? Isn't that the most important thing, to be with someone who makes you laugh? Maybe, if I could just get Asher to laugh with me, I could get him to fall for me. If only it were that easy, if only one good knock-knock joke was all it took.

Seeta aur Geeta

After midterms are over the junior class goes on a field trip to see *Romeo and Juliet* in the oval-shaped theater in Albany. I have to hand in a French assignment before we leave, and by the time I'm outside, the school bus that Bridget and Helena are on is already full, so I board the second one. Heather Esposito and her friends are sitting in the very back, and Ricca Rimes and Cassie Banks, whose parents co-own the only car dealership in Deer Hook, are sitting together in the middle. Ricca has green eyes and princess hair, long and silky and dark blond, and walks with a slight limp. Cassie has thin hair and big ears that stick out through her hair at a sharp angle. She's the captain of the girls' volleyball team and is probably the most athletic girl in school. Once I overheard Shannon Kelly saying that it was a shame you couldn't put Ricca's head on top of Cassie's body, and all the other guys were, like, yeah, how awesome would that be. That is the level of maturity of the boys at Deer Hook High.

As the bus begins to pull away, a voice yells, "Wait!" Asher is running toward us, his hair bouncing in artful waves about his head. The bus driver hits the brakes. After Asher boards he takes a moment to catch his breath, surveying the bus, and we make eye contact. He starts walking down the aisle. There are a few empty seats, but every molecule in my body is suddenly buzzing with the notion that Asher is heading to the empty seat next to me. He passes the first row, the second row, the third. Oh, my God. What am I going to do if Asher Richelli sits down next to me? Now he's two rows away, and his pace slows. *Oh*, my God.

Asher stops right in front of me. "Hey, Nina," he says.

I nod, mistrustful of how my voice will sound in a moment like this.

"Can I have the window?" he asks.

"Sure," I say, and get up. I can't believe this is happening.

"I bet you aced the math midterm. You seem like that kind of girl."

I can't tell how he feels about that kind of girl, so I remain silent. I tell myself to say something witty and engaging, but I can't think of anything, not a single question, not even a stupid knock-knock joke. "How do you think you did?" I ask. Ugh. I sound like I'm vying for the Most Boring Conversationalist of the Year Award.

"Okay, I guess." He pulls *Romeo and Juliet* out of his coat pocket. "I want to finish it before we get there," he says, opening it to a page toward the end.

I pull *Jane Eyre* out of my backpack. This is like the fifth time I'm reading it, and I can't focus on it anyway because Asher Richelli is less than a foot away from me, plus I get a little sick reading on buses. As I pretend to read I give myself a lecture. Nina Khan, you're supposed to be getting over this boy. Don't flirt with him, then hope his friendly response means something more than it does and be sad when it doesn't. Asher yawns and stretches out his arms and his legs, the way people do in the movies when they want to put their arm around someone, and I hold my breath. Of course he doesn't put his arm around me, but he does say, "So how come I never see you at any of the parties?"

"I don't go out much."

"You stay home and study on the weekends, huh?" Asher says, but he doesn't seem to be making fun of me. In fact, maybe I'm crazy, but there's a hint of admiration in his voice.

"Yeah, I suppose." I don't bother explaining that the real reason I don't go out is because I'm a Pakistani Muslim girl. "And I guess you spend a lot of your time hanging out with Serena."

"Yeah, I have been," he says. "But that might change soon."

Might change soon? At best, it's foreshadowing an imminent breakup; at the very least, it's not the response of someone who is truly in love. This is it—the moment my heart has been longing for, and now all I have to do is show him how funny and smart and irresistible I am. But I can't think of anything to say. I could ask him if he's had any more nightmares about sine and cosine, but I don't want to risk embarrassing him. What do you talk about with someone you hardly know? The weather and movies, of course. Asher's gazing out the window intently, like he's trying to memorize the landscape. I wonder if I should interrupt him, and decide I must. Us sitting next to each other is nothing less than fate. If I don't take advantage of this, I will regret it forever. One, two, three, *go*.

"So have you seen any good movies lately?" I say, and then remember how I saw Asher cuddling with Serena at the last movie I attended.

Asher snaps out of his repose, shakes his head. "No, not really. Have you?"

"Yeah," I say.

"Like what?" Asher turns so he's facing me. The boy I like is suddenly giving me his full attention, and my mind goes blank. I can't remember the name of the Asher-Serena make-out movie, or any other movie I've seen in the last year, for that matter, and end up blurting out, "*Seeta aur Geeta*." It's an old Bollywood movie, one of my favorite movies when I was young, and I can't believe I just said it.

"Seeta or what?" Asher asks.

"It's an Indian movie," I explain, resisting the urge to punch myself for being such an idiot. The last thing I need to do is emphasize the fact that I am a brown girl to the gentleman who prefers blondes.

"What is it about?"

Oh, boy. "Umm . . . it's about these twins separated at birth, Seeta and Geeta. Seeta is rich but her family is mean to her and treats her like a servant, except for her grandmother, who's bedridden, and Geeta is a street performer raised by a gypsy woman. Then one day

Seeta runs away from home and tries to kill herself and this guy who saves her thinks she's Geeta and she ends up having to be a street performer. And Geeta gets mistaken for Seeta and moves into Seeta's house and starts bossing around all of the relatives, but then she gets found out. And then Seeta gets abducted—" I stop. There is no way Asher can be following this.

"Sounds really complicated," he says. "Is that where your parents are from, India?"

"No, they're from Pakistan—it's a country right next to India."

"Yeah, I know where it is," Asher says. "Do your parents miss it?"

"Yeah. We're going to visit in December. Do your parents miss Italy?"

"My father likes it fine here, but my mother weeps for Pisa all the time."

"Well, Pisa must be a whole lot better than Deer Hook."

"That's not saying much, is it?"

He laughs and I do too. When he laughs his legs spread apart and his right leg touches mine for a brief second before returning to his half of the seat.

"I really should finish this before we get there," he says, holding up his book.

Could our brief knee kiss have been more than mere accident? Is Asher really going to break up with Serena? I try to stay calm as happy love endorphins explode like fireworks inside my body. Everything around me, the green vinyl of the seats, the gray of the floor, has become pastel and beautiful. I wonder how our return-address labels will read. Asher and Nina Richelli. Nina Khan-Richelli and Asher

Richelli. Nina Khan and Asher Richelli. They will have puppies or flowers on them, or maybe both.

Asher puts his book down. "Look." He points out the window. "Downtown."

I lean across him to look out the window at the Albany skyline, which consists of a couple of tall buildings and is not much to look at. I'm wearing a sweater that's a size too big on me and the manner in which I lean across him must give Asher a view down the back because when I sit up, he turns to me, one eyebrow raised in curious amusement.

"You have a stripe of hair going down your back," he says. And then he chuckles.

I press my spine into the seat. I'm so mortified I can't even look at him. I tell myself to remain cool and not act like I'm so mortified. What he said must be true; it's not the kind of thing you would say to someone if it wasn't. I wonder if I should reply, but how do you respond to something like this? I stay quiet, praying my face isn't too red with embarrassment, and pretend to look for something in my backpack until we finally get to where we're going.

Skunk Girl

As soon as I make it home I run upstairs to my room and tear my clothes off. I stand naked in front of my full-length mirror and twist my head to get a good view of my back. And that's when I see it. A wide line of soft, dark hair running from the nape of my neck down to the base of my spine—the stripe Asher was talking about. A stripe right down the center of my back, like a skunk. This brings me to a whole other level. I'm not just a hairy Pakistani Muslim girl anymore.

I am a skunk girl.

Upon a Star

I lie down on the floor, still naked, and cry into my pillow. After I cry, I curse. First I curse Allah for doing this to me. Then I just curse, yelling four-letter words into the pillow. When I tire of the crying and cursing, I maneuver my body around to try to see how much of the stripe is within reach, and much of it isn't, which means I can't wax, bleach, or shave it. My current methods of attack are useless. I am going to be a skunk girl for a while.

But no one really sees your back, I console myself. So, I can't wear a bikini. It's not like I ever go to the beach anyway. So, I can't go to second base with a guy. It's not as though I've ever gotten to first. The fact that I'm a skunk girl won't really affect my day-to-day life.

But whatever chance I had with Asher, however small, is now gone. Now I am, in his mind, forever tainted by this stripe, like a scarlet letter stamped on my spine. I wish I didn't have to see him again, ever. I imagine him pointing his finger at my back, with a smile that becomes increasingly mocking with each passing second. Then a thought stabs my brain, like I ran headfirst into a barbed-wire fence. What if Asher tells Serena?

I would be the most made-fun-of student in Deer Hook High history. I would be an outcast. Ostracized. People would stare at me like they stare at circus freaks, not the polite pretend-not-to-stare stares, but the full-on "oh my god look at you" stares. Have you seen the skunk girl? they'd ask their friends. And Serena . . . I can't even bring myself to think about all of the things Serena could say and do. It's too much.

I close my eyes and wish some more. I wish my mother would decide to homeschool me, starting tomorrow. I wish we would move to another state.

My kindergarten teacher told us that wishes that don't come true float up to the sky and sit on top of the clouds, and when the clouds become too heavy from the weight of these wishes, it rains. That night, I make so many wishes that I wouldn't have been surprised if a monsoon struck Deer Hook as I slept, flooding the streets and canceling school. I wish.

Rabbit Hole

The next morning, I'm still wishing. But no rabbit hole appears beneath my feet to help me disappear, nor does the bus driver suddenly announce he's turning the bus around and taking us to Canada. Walking into school I wait for someone to see me and point, and for others to turn and stare and burst into terrible laughter. But nothing happens. No one pauses their conversations. No one even notices me.

"Hey!" Bridget taps me on the shoulder. She's wearing a bright red wool sweater that looks itchy and uncomfortable. If my inner shame was a garment, her sweater would definitely be it. "Look what

Anthony gave me," she says, pulling her hair back to reveal a gold heart-shaped pendant.

"Have you heard any rumors about me?" I ask her.

"No. Why would there be a rumor about you?"

"Do you have to act *so* incredulous?"

She narrows her eyes. "Have you done something?"

"No, of course not."

"Is there something you're not telling me?"

I sense her before I see her—Serena heading down the hall with a few other people. There's a sharp pain in my stomach like someone just stapled it. She says hi to Bridget, but, aside from her obligatory nose-wrinkle, ignores me and continues past us down the hall.

I exhale. If Serena did know, there's no way she would have been able to hide it so well. She's about as subtle as the sweater Bridget's wearing. She must not know, which means Asher must not have said anything to anyone. Please, Allah, don't let Asher say anything to anyone. Ever.

"I'm not hiding anything, promise," I tell Bridget, and take off before she can interrogate me further.

Later, when I walk in late to precalc, I manage to avoid making eye contact with Asher, but of course I see him again at lunch, standing near the entrance to the cafeteria. I position myself between Bridget and Helena and pretend to be absorbed in their conversation, though I'm so nervous I have no idea what they're saying.

"Hey, Nina," Asher says, flashing me a smile as we walk past.

I focus on the floor, but then Bridget elbows me in the back so hard I pitch forward a bit.

"Easy there," Asher says, and I can't get inside the cafeteria fast enough.

"Have I told you how much I hate you?" I snap at Bridget.

"Whatever!" Bridget puts her hands on both of my shoulders and starts speaking in this serious tone that reminds me of Sonia. "Listen to me. If a boy you like says hi to you, you say hi back. Got it?"

"I don't know if I like him anymore," I say.

Bridget makes her annoyed face, eyes wide, lips pursed, like she's going to pretend to kiss you but then bites your nose off instead. "Suit yourself!" she says, and stomps to the lunch line.

I think about the way Asher smiled at me. It seemed genuinely friendly, nothing crooked or malicious about it. In fact, nothing in his mannerism suggested that just yesterday he discovered something freakishly embarrassing about me. Could he have forgotten? That didn't seem possible. More likely, he's taken pity on me, decided that he's obliged to be nice to me because of my flaw. But that's fine with me; I'll take pity over disgust any day.

The Damn Goat

Our lunchtime trio has expanded, with Vinny and Anthony joining us at least twice a week. "We should be in a Benetton ad," Helena comments on one of the days the five of us are at the table.

"Please. The last thing I need is to advertise my fifth-wheel status on a giant billboard," I say.

"Who cares? At least you'll be on a billboard," Bridget says.

"We need to find you a man," Anthony says.

"Nina already has a man in mind," Bridget tells him.

"Not him." Anthony shakes his head. Great. Bridget has obviously blabbered the details of my forlorn love life to her boyfriend. "You need a real man," he continues. "Someone who truly appreciates you." Bridget squeezes his arm and flashes an "oh my god my boyfriend is so sensitive and yet so strong" smile.

"Maybe guys don't appreciate Nina because she's not allowed to date," Vinny offers. "I mean, why lust after the whiskey that's in a locked cabinet when you can walk down to the store and buy a bottle?"

"That's not very helpful, Vinny," Helena says, which it isn't. She's no closer to breaking up with him than she was a few weeks ago. She claims that she can see Vinny becoming more confident, more focused, and after a little more time together, she hopes he'll be ready to be on his own again.

"I was just making a point," Vinny says. He takes a plum out of his lunch bag and stares at it.

"Why so glum, plum?" Anthony says. Though his quips aren't always funny, I give him an A for enthusiasm, like my father. I bet the two of them would get along.

Vinny puts the plum back in his lunch bag. Helena frowns at the ceiling. I decide to change the subject. "Aren't you cold in that?" I ask Anthony. He's wearing a T-shirt, the sleeves snug around his biceps.

"I'm always hot," Anthony responds. "I've got the islands in my veins."

"He says he even gets hot inside movie theaters in the middle of summer," Bridget says.

"Speaking of islands, what are you eating today?" I ask. Anthony usually brings leftovers from home, yummy things like callaloo and spicy stews.

"Goat curry," he replies. "You want some?"

"Yes, please. We eat goat too," I tell him. "I love it."

"I should be dating her," Anthony says, pushing his curry across the table toward me.

Bridget punches his arm. "You also eat pig snout," she says. "Nina can't eat pork."

"No pork, no boyfriends," I say, sighing dramatically. "I think I deserve the rest of this curry." It's really good, richly spiced with a peppery flavor. If there's one thing nonwhites have over white people, it's food.

"I'll try some too," Vinny says, and I push the goat curry over to him.

"Since when do you eat goat?" Helena asks.

"I don't. I want to know what it tastes like." Vinny's fork pauses in midair. "You think I shouldn't try it?"

"No, if you want to try it, you should," Helena says.

"I won't try it if you don't want me to," he replies.

"It's good to try new things, Vinny."

"Are you sure you don't mind?" he asks.

"Just try the damn goat!" Bridget snaps. Patience has never been one of her virtues.

Vinny takes a bite. "It's good." He offers his fork to Helena. "Do you want to try some?"

"I'm okay, thanks," Helena says.

"You're not upset that I had some, are you?" he asks.

"Of course not," she tells him. "I love it when you take ownership of your actions." Vinny smiles and retrieves the plum from his bag. Next thing you know she'll be writing Vinny a self-help manual. Maybe someone could write me a self-help manual. *How to Embrace Yourself and Stop Wishing Your Life Away.* After all, I am who I am and I look how I look and I have to learn to accept it. Accepting yourself, though challenging, seems achievable. Actually embracing yourself seems like the tough part.

At the end of the day I see Asher outside, leaning against the Henry Hudson statue. I've seen him standing here before, waiting for Serena. It's excellent positioning for him; the bronze of the statue brings out the olive tones in his skin, making him even darker and sexier. It makes him seem like he doesn't belong here. It's as though he fell asleep in the Mediterranean and woke up in Deer Hook. "Hey, Nina," he calls out.

"Hi," I say.

"How come you still take the bus?" he asks.

"My dad's still teaching me how to drive."

"I can give you a ride home, sometimes," he offers.

I ought to be flying right now, but since the incident on the bus I feel so uncomfortable around him. Whenever I talk to him my shame is like a ghost, hovering in the pauses of our dialogue. How can you have a normal conversation with someone who knows your horrible secret?

"I can't," I tell him. "My parents would flip if they saw me in some guy's car. They're strict like that."

Asher nods. "Like real old-school Italians, huh?"

"Yeah, kind of," I say, though aside from my father's fondness for carbs and cheese, it's probably not the most apt comparison. "I have to catch my bus."

Asher is still leaning against Henry Hudson's legs as the bus pulls away. I watch him for as long as possible, and then realize how I would seem if he were to see me now, my cheek pressed against the window of a yellow school bus filled with lower classmen, staring at him like I've never seen a cute boy before. I move away from the window. The back of the seat in front of me is ripped in several places and in the center someone has written "S ♥ G." I take my pen and scribble out the heart. Maybe it's an awful thing to do, but between being a fifth wheel at lunch and feeling so ashamed when I talk to Asher, I can't bear witness to anyone else's love right now, even if it is just scrawled across peeling vinyl.

Even the Mean Girls

It's happened. Asher has dumped Serena. Serena is crying in front of the entrance to the bathroom surrounded by girls, including Bridget, who has one hand on Serena's shoulder and whose other hand gives me a discreet thumbs-up as I walk past. Serena skulks around school, teary-eyed, and insists on having dramatic, public embraces with every one of her current and former girlfriends, even if they've barely spoken since seventh grade. In English class she stares straight ahead, and keeps drawing circles over and over in her notebook until there's no white space left on the page. She may be annoying and superficial and mean, and it is comforting to know that even the mean girls get their hearts broken, but she looks so pathetic I can't help but feel a little sorry for her.

When Helena sees me in the hall she raises her hand for a high-five. "You must be thrilled. Asher is single again!"

"I can't say I'm not a little pleased. But I'm trying to keep it in perspective—it's not like he's going to stay single for long." Already the girls in our school are sharpening their claws, preparing to pounce.

"Nina!" The high-five turns into an accusatory finger-jab. "Why do you always have to be so negative? Don't you know that positive things are much more likely to happen to positive people?"

Positive things happen to pretty, desirable people like Helena, but I don't say this, because she would insist that I'm pretty and desirable too.

"Furthermore," she continues, "I heard Cassie Banks saying that she overheard Asher saying that he doesn't want to get back into a relationship anytime soon. That'll give you some time to get to know him better. I know you can't date him really, but you never know. Maybe it could work, somehow."

I know Helena believes this, but she doesn't understand that it's almost cruel to try to make me believe it too. "Break up with Vinny yet?" I ask, and she stamps her foot.

"Fine, be that way," she says. "But let me ask you this—if you keep insisting that the glass is half empty, why do you even bother to thirst?"

Helena storms off before I can respond. Why do I bother to thirst? I thirst because I'm sixteen and full of hormones and because sometimes when Asher smiles the left side of his lips lifts higher than the right. Maybe Helena is right. Even if I end up being disappointed, having a little bit of hope wouldn't kill me. Just a little bit—if I imagine too much water in my glass, I could end up drowning in it.

Once Upon a Lint

Deer Hook High has a winter formal every December. This year it's a Sadie Hawkins dance and even though it's almost a month away practically half the girls in school are talking about how they'd love to go with Asher. Some of them have even begun their not-so-stealthy maneuvers. Nearly every time I see him in school a different girl is talking to him, and Asher is so friendly to all of them it's hard to tell if he likes one in particular. "He says he needs time," I overhear Laura McNutt say. "Isn't that the sweetest thing?" According to Bridget, Serena is pissed at any girl who flirts with Asher, which means she's pissed at practically every girl in school, including most of her friends. This explains why she's been talking to Bridget and Helena a lot lately, since she doesn't have to worry about them going after her ex.

I'm leaving my locker when I hear Asher calling out my name behind me. I haven't spoken with him since last week, when he offered me a ride home. It occurs to me that, except for the fateful one on the bus, most of our conversations have centered around academics. Which makes sense, I guess. I mean, that's pretty much my image—Nina who does well in school and not much else. But at least I'm not as self-conscious anymore when I talk to him. I feel pretty confident now that he's not going to tell anyone about my stripe, and since it doesn't seem to bother him that I've got one, I'm trying hard not to let it bother me. As long as he never ever brings it up again. The day he does that, I'll die. "How are you?" Asher asks when he catches up to me.

"I'm all right, I guess."

He raises his eyebrows. "You guess?"

Great. Way to present myself as someone uncertain about her own well-being. I change the topic. "How are you doing? Word on the street is that you're going to lead the basketball team to the state finals in the spring."

"We have a pretty solid team, so it's possible." Asher has too much humility to sing his own praises, though maybe it's easier to have humility when the entire school is singing your praises for you.

I think of something else to say. "Are you looking forward to winter formal?"

"Yeah, I suppose. You?"

"I can't go."

"Right," Asher nods. "Your parents."

He has a piece of white lint in his hair and I debate whether or not to tell him this. Asher and I are sort of friends, and that's what friends do, right? But before I can say anything the bell rings and Asher says bye and walks away. Now some other girl will get to tell him that he has something in his hair and maybe even pull it out for him, and maybe he'll be so grateful that when she asks him out he'll say yes. Maybe our entire future turns upon that one piece of lint, and I've officially missed the only chance I'll ever have.

The Wisdom of Grandmothers

L isten," Bridget says to me as we head to lunch. "Serena asked if she could eat with us today."

"I hope you said no."

"Come on, Nina. She's been having a hard time and apparently she told her friends that they had to choose between her and Asher, and half of them decided they preferred flirting with Asher."

"How tragic."

"I have an idea—why don't you stop being so nasty and give her a chance?"

"*I'm* nasty? How did I become the bad guy in this situation? Or is your memory so selective it can't recall how Serena has treated me?"

Bridget shakes her head. "I don't know what you mean. You guys hardly talk! And I don't even know if she's actually going to sit with us, so don't have a conniption just yet."

It's true that Serena and I hardly talk, but Bridget has conveniently forgotten the legacy of Serena's occasional cruel acts toward me when we were younger. *Par exemple*, Bridget's birthday party, third grade. We were all gathered in Bridget's basement. I had about four glasses of orange soda and I went to use the bathroom, which was close to where all the guests were sitting. While I was in there, I heard Serena exclaiming, "Listen, you can hear Nina peeing!" and everyone, everyone being most of our third grade class, started laughing. I stopped what I was doing and tried not to cry. When I came back out people snickered and Helena picked up the baseball bat and said, "Let's break the piñata!" because she could tell how mortified I was. I still had to use the bathroom, but I was too scared, and by the time the party ended and I'd finally reached the safety of my house, I'd already gone a little bit in my underwear. And Bridget says she doesn't know what I mean.

At lunch, it's Helena, Bridget, Anthony, and me. No sign of Serena. "Tell us, lovebirds, how did it go?" Helena asks. She's referring to the fact that Anthony met Bridget's parents last night.

"My parents were really cool about it," Bridget says.

"They were all right," Anthony says.

Bridget punches him. "What are you talking about? They loved you!"

"Well," Anthony begins, "I go over there, and her father sits me down and gives me the third degree. What do my parents do, what kind of grades do I get, do I want to go to college, do I have a career in mind?"

"Sounds scary," I say. Although, if my parents did allow me to date, I could see my father doing the same thing, with maybe a few dumb jokes thrown in if the guy was lucky.

"Anyway, once he established that I was a respectable young black man, he was fine. But I don't know if he would have given me the third degree like that if I was white."

"Maybe, maybe not," Bridget says. "But Anthony really did impress them. Before he came over, they were telling me how they had nothing against interracial relationships, but other people might. My mom was hinting that sometimes it's better to take the easier path, but then after he left she said she understood how I couldn't resist him."

"Therefore, being respectable and irresistible makes up for being black," Anthony adds.

"They're not like that! They really liked you. Even my little brother, who's rude to everyone, liked you," Bridget protests. "You should have seen him charming my mom and dad. 'Why, Mrs. McPherson, this is the best brisket I've ever tasted,' " she says, imitating Anthony's deep voice. "What can I say? The boy sells himself. If he was a piece of turd he'd get someone to buy him."

"Bridget!" Helena cries, and as we're laughing, Serena approaches.

"Hi, Serena! Would you like to join us?" Helena offers, as if Bridget hadn't already told her that Serena might show up.

Serena smiles, all sweet and grateful, the big fraud. "Thanks. She sits down across from me, button nose staying perfectly still. "Hi, everyone." Everyone says hi back, but I just nod. She takes out a grapefruit from her lunch bag and starts peeling it with her pink nails. "Would anyone like a slice?"

Anthony makes a face like she's offered us a slice of lye. "No, thanks," Helena says. Serena looks at me. "Nina, do you want some grapefruit?"

Of course—I'm the only person she asks by name because I'm the person at the table who can stand to lose the most weight. "I'm good."

She's still looking at me. "How are you?" she asks. "I feel like I only see you in English class."

Bridget and Helena and Anthony watch us intently, a rapt audience as Serena and I play out our twisted comedy of manners. "I'm fine," I reply, and then I decide I should hit the ball back to her side of the court. "How are *you* doing?"

She sighs. "It started out as the best semester of my life and it's turned into the worst."

"Well, you look great," Bridget says.

"That's because I stopped eating." She puts down the half-peeled grapefruit. "It wouldn't be so hard if I didn't have to watch girls like Laura McNutt hurling themselves at him like, like cannonballs."

"Oh, Serena." Helena puts her arm around her and Serena leans on her shoulder and starts rubbing her eyes, probably in an attempt to make herself cry. "You have to be strong."

"You're much hotter than Laura," Anthony tells her.

Serena smiles. "You are too sweet, Anthony, really."

"If Asher decides to go to winter formal with Laura McNutcase, he's a fool," Bridget says.

He is not a fool! I want to yell. Dumping Serena was his best off-court move of the year. But Laura McNutt? She's a cheerleader, a blonde, albeit a fake one, and she has big boobs as well. Will he ever realize there are other instruments in the orchestra besides the cymbal? I hope no one told him about that piece of lint in his hair. I hope it grows and grows until you can't even see his hair for all the lint.

"I was so dumb," Serena whimpers, an actual tear falling from her eye. "I never should have believed it when he said he loved me."

Asher said he loved her?

"Don't think like that," Helena says, stroking her hair.

"Forget about Laura McButt," Bridget orders. "And stop crying. What if Asher sees you? Where's your pride, girl? This isn't the Serena I know!"

Serena wipes her face with her napkin. "You're right."

"What you need to think about is who you want to ask to Sadie Hawkins," Helena says.

Serena shakes her head. "I hate this whole ask-a-guy thing. This Sadie chick must have been a sadist." I'm impressed that she knows such a big word. I think she might be able to read my mind because as soon as I think this she looks at me. "Are you asking anyone, Nina?"

"I can't go," I say.

The button nose scrunches. "Really? I can't believe your parents won't even let you go to Sadie Hawkins." The tears have ceased. She's no doubt thrilled that there's someone at the table whose life is more pathetic than hers. "It's the biggest event of the semester. Maybe your parents don't understand that."

Before I can even say anything, I feel Bridget's thumb pressing into my spine. She wants me to remain calm, and I do. "I don't think that argument will work with my parents. But it's okay. I've never been allowed to go to dances. I'm used to it."

"Formals are overrated," pronounces Helena. She would know since she's been to every one since ninth grade.

"That's true, but I'm still looking forward to it," Bridget says, winking at Anthony.

I spend the rest of the day annoyed that Asher might have told Serena he loved her and wondering what my life would be like had I been born a white girl. Then I'd have a mother who'd help me buy a prom dress and a father who'd take pictures of me and my date posing on our porch, and maybe I'd be the kind of girl Asher Richelli could fall in love with.

I'm sitting on the bench outside the entrance to the gym after school, killing time before my Volunteer Society meeting, when Anthony comes up to me. "Why so glum, plum?" he asks.

"Do you ever wish you were white?" I inquire. "Because right now, I think if someone offered me the chance to live my life again as a cute blonde, I would take it in a heartbeat."

Anthony shakes his head. "My grandmother used to say, 'If a man got everything he wished for, he'd end up one miserable son of a bitch.' "

"Your grandmother said that?"

Anthony nods and sits down next to me. "Anyway, what makes you so certain you'd be happier if you were white? How do you know you wouldn't end up thinking about the things you left behind? Like your family or the food you grew up eating or your pride?"

"I know. But it just seems like it would be so much easier."

Anthony pats my knee. He's got nice hands, broad with deep pink nails. "My grandmother used to say, 'True beauty never comes from easy.' "

"Your grandmother sounds like quite a woman."

"Yeah, she was. She's the one that made me that schwa sweatshirt." He squints up at the ceiling. "She used to have an answer for everything, then she got Alzheimer's. When she died she didn't even know her own name."

"Is that why you used to wear that schwa sweatshirt every day?"

Anthony smiles. "I wore it because it was fly. But, yeah, maybe that was part of it too."

Bridget appears in front of us. "What's up, hot buns?" she says to Anthony, sliding into his lap.

"Just sitting here having a chat with Nina," he tells her, caressing her cheek with his finger. She pretends to bite it, and he laughs and kisses her, and suddenly there's this knot in my stomach. Though I am really happy Bridget has found love, the truth is that right that second, I'm more jealous than I am happy.

Marriage, Not Colonizers

S onia comes home for Thanksgiving. She seems even more petite than when I last saw her, which probably means that I've grown bigger.

"Hi," I say.

"Act like sisters!" my mother cries, pushing us together. We hug loosely and separate.

"Every time I come home Dad has less and less hair," Sonia says, rubbing his head.

"I miss my daughter so much my hair keeps falling out," my father says, and Sonia vanishes momentarily inside his arms.

"I have so much studying to do," Sonia complains. She always spends Thanksgiving holed up in her room, reviewing for her finals, even though they're not until after Christmas break. She'll probably bring her textbooks with her on our trip to Pakistan and be holed up in some room over there the whole time. "Can we have Pakistani food for Thanksgiving dinner?" she asks. "I'm sick of American food."

"But I already bought a turkey," my mother says.

"Make masala turkey!" my father says.

My mom made masala turkey once, marinated overnight in Pakistani spices. I'm not a fan. Some things, like turkey and hamburgers, are not meant to be spicy. "But I hate masala turkey," I protest, and everyone ignores me. Sonia has spoken, therefore we will have Pakistani food for Thanksgiving dinner, even though the rest of us eat Pakistani food every day.

My mother spends Thanksgiving day cooking some of Sonia's favorite dishes: goat meat cooked with spinach, Afghani *biryani* with carrots and raisins, kheer pudding with sliced almonds, and, of course, the masala turkey.

After we sit at the table, my father says grace. "Oh, Allah, thank you for our health and our happiness and our two lovely daughters, and may you always guide us down the right path. *Bismillah.*" He rubs his hands together. "Let's eat!" he exclaims, his face glowing at the juxtaposition of his two great loves—his family, whole again, and my mother's cooking.

As we eat, Sonia spends half an hour talking about how hard her organic chemistry lab is and how she'd love to go to Harvard Med but she doesn't think she'll get in because even if she aces her MCAT, her science GPA isn't quite high enough.

"That's fine, Sonia," my mother says. "We know you have worked hard and will get into a good medical school. But there is more to life than grades, you know."

Not to a supernerd.

"Samina Auntie has a nephew," my mother continues.

Sonia and I both stop eating.

"He is a first-year medical student at Georgetown Medical School. A little dark, but from a very nice family. If you like I can give him your number."

"I'm only nineteen!" Sonia says, waving her right hand in the air. A grain of rice that was clinging to her fingers flies off and lands on my plate.

"If you want to get married in your twenties you need to start thinking about it now."

"But I have to focus solely on my studies for the next few years." She turns to my father. "Right, Dad?"

My father shrugs. "Of course you should focus on your studies, but one day you must also get married. The worst fate is to be a woman alone."

My mother reaches over and takes my father's hand. "Your father and I understand that your generation has different ideas about marriage and it is okay with us if you find a nice Pakistani boy on your own. But we think he should be a doctor as well, so you two will be on equal footing professionally—a nondoctor husband might get an inferiority complex. And he shouldn't be *too* dark."

It has never been clear to me how dark is too dark. Pakistanis are very impressed by light skin, so much so that my mother spends ten minutes putting on sunscreen before she leaves the house, and never allowed Sonia and me to play any outdoor sports because she didn't want us to "ruin" our complexions.

Sonia shakes her head. "Spare me the too-dark nonsense. Why do you insist on adopting this colonizer mentality?"

"We're talking about your marriage, not colonizers," my mother says.

"So, isn't this e-mail thing awesome?" Sonia asks. "It's going to change the world as we know it. You guys should really think about getting it."

My mother frowns. "Stop trying to switch the subject. All we are asking is that you keep your eyes open for nice boys. The good ones always get snapped up quickly. You don't want to be twenty-six and single and stuck with the ones nobody wants."

My mother is talking about boys as if they are products sold at a department store. I can tell by the way Sonia's cheeks are puffed up that she is annoyed and about to start a diatribe of some kind, but something makes her decide against it, and the cheeks deflate. "I'll make sure to keep an eye out," she says.

"Good girl," my mother replies, and Sonia stares into the depths of her water glass.

Fun House Mirrors

For the rest of the weekend I see Sonia at dinner, and Friday night we all watch a Bollywood movie together, but most of the time she stays in her room, working, and I stay in mine, pretending to work. It's not as though Sonia and I were ever close. She spent all of her time studying and then she was gone. But now that my love life has sunken as low as nonexistent love lives can possibly sink, it occurs to me that Sonia might be the only person who can relate to the pathos of my social life and maybe offer advice on how to make it through high school without going mad, and on Saturday I knock on her door.

"Come in!" she yells.

Sonia's room is a mess. There are books scattered everywhere, on the floor, on her bed, stacked on her dresser and in her closet, MCAT books and textbooks of different colors and sizes, novels, science journals, and, to my surprise, a women's fashion magazine. The only neat thing is her bed. Sonia is particular about certain things, and one of them is her bed. The blanket has to be folded down once and tucked in under the mattress, and every stuffed animal has to be in a row against the wall from oldest to most recent. She's lying down next to the animals, reading a book that rests upright on her chest. I could never read lying on my back like she does.

"What's up?" she says. "Is Ma calling me?"

"No." I don't even know where to begin, and for some reason I spit out something that has nothing to do with either friends or love. "I hate being hairy."

Sonia doesn't flinch. She takes a bookmark from her nightstand and places it carefully in her book. "Oh, Ma will let you start electrolysis when you go to college. I've been doing it for two years now and my mustache is completely gone."

"It's just that it's so embarrassing," I say, wondering how many years it would take to "electrolysize" my stripe.

"It's not that bad. There are much worse things to be, like stupid. And think of it this way—it may be considered a flaw, but it's a flaw you can get rid of. Imagine if you had a permanent flaw instead, like a huge scar across your face or some other kind of disfigurement."

This may be a true statement, but it doesn't make me feel much better when I spend my days surrounded by girls who are neither hairy nor disfigured. "Sometimes I don't know how I'm going to last the next year and a half in Deer Hell High," I say.

Sonia sits up, cross-legged, folds her arms, and starts speaking in her serious-supernerd voice, which is a bit lower than her regular voice and utilizes a lot of pauses for emphasis.

"Now, Nina," she says. "The point of high school is to do well so you can get into a good college. Just concentrate on your studies and ignore everything else."

"But I'm not like you. I'm not that into studying. I mean, I am, but not the way you were in high school."

Sonia sighs, pushes her glasses up, and thinks for a moment. "Remember Vithu Duong?"

"Yes."

"For four years in high school I was completely obsessed with doing better in school than he did. Now we're both at Harvard, and I saw him once my very first semester, and I haven't seen him since. We've become inconsequential to each other. What I am trying to say is that when you grow up in a place like Deer Hook you perceive your life through one of those fun house mirrors, the kind that makes things that are small seem gargantuan. It's all about perspective. One day you might even look back on your high school years fondly."

"Only because I'll be glad they're over," I say.

"Really? What about Bridget and Helena?" she asks.

"What about them?"

"Don't you think you're lucky to have two such close friends? Ma told me how they surprised you for your birthday. I wish I had had friends like that in high school."

She has a point. I can't imagine my life, let alone high school, without Bridget and Helena, and it makes me sad that one day we'll go our separate ways to college and, though I'm sure we'll always stay close, it might never be the same again.

"What are you thinking?" Sonia asks.

"Oh, nothing. I suppose I will be able to survive the next year and a half."

"Of course you will. Focus on the positive and keep your eye on the prize," Sonia says.

By "prize" I assume she means an Ivy League school. "Thanks for the advice," I say. "By the way, when Nasreen Khala was here she reminded Ma that when her daughter was your age, she was already engaged. I think that's part of the reason Ma's so riled up about marriage."

Sonia groans. "I'm not even a senior yet!" She shakes her head and opens up her book. "Anyway, feel free to knock anytime you want to talk."

She's going back to Harvard tomorrow, and this is probably the only sister talk we'll have, but it's a nice offer, all the same. I smile at her and she smiles back, and it reminds me that one thing we definitely have in common is our nose, our mother's nose, thin at the top and wide at the bottom, with nostrils that flare slightly whenever we smile.

The First Unicorn

Mr. Porcupine decides to give our whole class a lecture. "I know I've mentioned this before, but I was very disappointed with your overall performance on the midterm. Some of you may think math is nothing more than an annoyance, but I still expect everyone to put real, honest effort into this class. You know, I once had a student who exercised such effort and intelligence that I wrote a more challenging midterm for her." He blinks a few times, perhaps holding back his nostalgic tears for that certain student who shall remain anonymous.

Asher starts walking next to me after class. He hasn't shaved in a few days and the stubble on his face is that perfect length. There's a Milky Way spot near the right side of his chin where his facial hair grows in a swirl, and I have an urge to press the tip of my index finger against it. "Can you believe that speech he gave?" he says. "I mean, was that supposed to inspire us?"

"I think that was the goal," I say.

"That student he was talking about, was that your sister? I heard she was some kind of genius."

I can't believe this. Even Asher has heard of my sister. With my luck, the next thing you know he'll be asking for her number, because he's decided that he's tired of blondes and wants to try dating a genius. "I don't know for certain if he was talking about her, but it's a pretty safe bet."

"It must be hard for you, always being compared to her," he says, and then puts his hand over his mouth for a second. "I didn't mean that you're not a genius, I meant—"

"It's okay. I'm fine with being a nongenius, really," I tell him. He's embarrassed; he's crinkling his forehead and there's a small depression between his eyebrows and he looks impossibly cute.

The bell rings. "I have to go to PE," I say. We're playing floor hockey these days, which I actually kind of enjoy. Hitting the puck hard with the stick is a nice stress reliever.

"See you later," he says. The forehead uncrinkles, the depression disappears, and so does he.

"Why does Asher only like blondes?" I complain at lunch the next day.

Bridget waves her straw at me. "What's wrong with blondes? I'm a blonde."

"There's nothing wrong with blondes, per se. It's just, you know, the cute boy in school dating the blondes. It's so cliché."

"I agree," says Helena.

"Hey, why isn't Vinny sitting with us at lunch anymore?" Bridget asks.

"I told him we needed to be more independent," Helena says.

"She's weaning him, like one of Serena's baby goats," I explain.

"I suppose I am," Helena admits. "I wish he didn't like me so much. Why are relationships so hard?"

"Speaking of relationships," Bridget says, "Anthony and I are going to have a romantic dinner together Friday night to celebrate my birthday. And then, we're going to do you know what."

"What?" I ask.

"Have sex, you moron," she says.

"Not have sex," Helena corrects her. "Make love."

"I didn't know you were planning on having sex with Anthony," I say.

Bridget leans back in her chair, and folds her arms. "It is time, girls, for this cherry to get popped."

"Bridget!" Helena cries. "Don't talk about it like that! When you have sex with someone you deeply love, it's a powerful, beautiful union."

"How are you feeling about it?" I ask Bridget.

"It's obvious, isn't it?" Helena says. "The more grandstanding Bridget does, the more nervous it means she is."

Bridget twists her arms together so they look like they're braided. "God, you can't even crack some jokes around here without getting psychoanalyzed. And yes, I am a little nervous, but I love Anthony and I trust him, so more than anything I'm feeling really good about it."

"You better use protection," I tell her.

"Don't worry," Bridget replies. "Nothing gets popped without a condom."

"Must you use that verb?" Helena asks. Bridget pretends to throw her straw at her and Helena ducks under the table. "Before I forget!" she says when she reemerges. "I've decided that, for Bridget's birthday, I'm going to host a sleepover at my house Saturday night. An old-fashioned sleepover, you know, like we used to have—us in our pajamas, doing our nails, eating pizza, watching scary movies. It'll be so fun. The witch said she'd bake cookies, and one of her cookies with a glass of milk is simply divine." Talk about irony— Bridget is about to leave innocence behind and Helena wants to return to it. "Nina, do you think there's any way you could come?"

"I doubt it. But it can't hurt to try, right?" I tell her. It sounds like fun. I love cookies and horror movies, and my mother doesn't like me to watch them at home. She gets so scared by the music she can't even make it through the opening credits.

"But what about Cassie's party? That's Saturday night too, and Anthony and I were planning on going," Bridget says.

"I'm sick of these high school parties where everyone gets drunk and acts stupid. They're so, so, *cliché*," Helena says. "But if you want to hang out with Anthony instead of coming to the birthday sleepover I'm planning in your honor, that's fine."

"What are you talking about? A girl can't miss her own birthday sleepover, can she?" Bridget says.

Helena hugs herself, excited. "Hooray! Who even needs a man when a girl has friends like you?"

I can appreciate the truth in this statement, but Bridget does one of her armpit farts.

"I'd advise you not to do that on the big night," Helena says, and Bridget turns red.

I can't believe Bridget is going to have sex. Whenever Helena refers to sex she might as well be talking about unicorns because she always describes it as something that is magical and powerful and precious. But Helena hasn't had sex yet; she's waiting until the right time, which is whenever she falls madly and passionately in love with the man of her dreams. I guess some people might not even require affection to have sex, and others, like Helena, demand a love like an ocean.

Permission Granted

That evening, my mother works late at the office and I wait for her to come home, thinking about how best to broach the subject of Helena's sleepover. She looks exhausted when she gets home, but after hours of nervous anticipation I can't back down now. "Helena is having a sleepover on Saturday night for Bridget's birthday. Can I go?"

My mother sits down on the couch and rests her feet on the ottoman. "Will you bring me the massager?"

I dig out her blue foot massager from the cabinet underneath the kitchen sink, fill it with hot water, and carry it over, carefully setting it next to her feet. "Ma? It's only girls and we're going to eat pizza and watch movies, nothing else. I really want to go. Can I please go?" I kneel down and start pressing her calves.

"Why don't you have the sleepover in our house?" The few times I've brought up sleepovers since the official ban freshman year, this has been her response. But there's no point in having a sleepover unless you can talk freely and loudly about boys.

"Because Helena's already planned it. And Ma, I can't live my whole life in our house."

"Nina, you know we don't feel comfortable with you staying over at other people's homes. If it was a nice Pakistani family, it would be different. But I'm sure Helena's father has beer in his fridge, and it's not right for a strange man to see you in your pajamas, and he has a girlfriend who lives with him." I wonder how she knows this, and she continues, "The business partner of Helena's father is one of your father's patients. You weren't going to tell me yourself that he lives with his girlfriend, were you? I know more than you think, Nina." This is a very frightening statement. She sighs again. "Poor Helena, first her mother leaves her, then a strange woman moves in. Is she nice to her?"

"Nice enough, I guess," I say. "Listen, we're going to spend the whole time in Helena's room and her father isn't going to see us in our pj's. Please?" I look up at her with eyes as wide and pleading as I can make them. "Please?" I plug in the massager. She eases each foot into the water and closes her eyes.

"You can go for a little bit," my mother says. "Midnight."

"One a.m.!" I say, and kiss her on the cheek, running away before she can change her mind.

Hold the Pork

My mother comes into my room on Friday night and tells me to get ready. "Put some nice clothes on. We're going out for dinner," she announces.

"What?" I say.

We almost never go out to dinner, at least not to nice restaurants. My mother thinks it's a waste of money and that nothing tastes as good as Pakistani food anyway. On the rare occasions we do go out she usually makes a face and proclaims the food bland or reminds us that nothing is better than her cooking.

"Where are we going?" I ask, hoping it's not Albany. I don't feel like sitting in the car for an hour just to have a meal.

"La Traviata," my mother says.

"La Traviata!" I exclaim. Of all the places! I think of an escape route. "I hate Italian food!"

"No, you don't," my mother replies.

My father walks in. Unlike my mother, my father doesn't mind spending money on food since eating is his favorite pastime. As soon as he enters the room he claps his hands not once, but twice. "Get ready, Nina!" he says. "We are having Italiano tonight."

"Why don't you two go? It would be nice, like a romantic date."

My father squeezes my shoulder. "Romance is having your whole family with you!"

Half an hour later we are in the car driving toward Main Street. My parents are in Western clothes. My father's wearing an off-white shirt, a navy argyle sweater vest, and khaki pants; my mother, black pants and a purple cashmere sweater. They look seminormal, and this gives me hope. Maybe dinner won't be so bad. And besides, maybe Asher won't even be there. He can't possibly work every Friday night.

When we walk in a young woman asks, "How many?" in a slight accent. I wonder if she's related to Asher, but she doesn't resemble him. She's short and pale, her light blond hair swept back with a red banana clip.

She seats us at a table in the back. The restaurant is cozy, with a brick fireplace, low ceilings, and dark red tablecloths and candles on every table. A mural on one of the walls depicts the Leaning Tower of Pisa next to a round, white building that looks like some kind of church. It's classy for Deer Hook, where the only other proper sit-down restaurants are the diner and the country club.

"And here is the wine menu," the hostess says, putting it down in the center of our table.

"We don't drink," my mother tells her, but she's already walked away.

My parents start discussing the menu choices and I do a quick scan of the room. The only staff I see are the hostess, an old waiter in a black bowtie, and a busboy. No sign of Asher. Reassured, I pick up my menu.

"Can I get you something to drink?"

I'd recognize that voice anywhere. There he is, Asher Richelli, standing in front of our table. Oh, my God.

"Hey, Nina!" he says.

"Hi."

"You should have told me you were coming," he tells me. "I would've gotten you a better table."

"Oh, this one is fine," I insist. My parents shift in their seats, no doubt alarmed by the familiar tone Asher is using with me, as if we're close friends or something. "This is Asher. He goes to my school."

My mother smiles. "Hello."

"Hello!" my father booms.

"It's very nice to meet you." Asher extends his hand. My father looks at it for a moment before shaking it. Asher removes the pen from behind his ear. "So, have you had a chance to look at our wine list?"

"Oh, no!" My father puts his hand up, palm facing out, like a crossing guard. "We don't drink."

"No alcohol," my mother adds, in case Asher didn't get it.

"We're Muslim," my father explains.

Asher nods, biting on the tip of his pen. "Do you want anything else to drink? Some soda, maybe?"

What I want is to crawl under the table and die, but that isn't a menu option. "I'll have a Coke," I say.

"Me too," my father adds.

"Water for me," my mother says.

"Two Cokes and a water," Asher repeats. "I'll be right back."

I wait until he's out of earshot before snapping. "You only have to say things once, you know. White people aren't stupid. They understand things the first time."

"We're only making sure," my father says, spreading his napkin over his lap. "Why so angry? Relax. Enjoy. Do we get any bread? I'm starving."

"He is a handsome boy," my mother says in Urdu.

"He's very popular in school," I respond.

As soon as I say this, Asher returns with our drinks and a basket of bread. My father goes straight for the bread, breaking off a hunk and spilling crumbs all over the tablecloth.

"Are you ready to order?" Asher asks.

"I'll have the shrimp *fra diavolo*," my mother tells him.

Asher turns to me. "And for you, Nina?" he says. God, he's such a charming waiter.

"Fettuccine Alfredo," I say, and immediately wonder whether I should have ordered a salad instead. Serena would never order a dish as fattening as fettuccine Alfredo, and he told her he loved her.

"And I'll have the veal parmigiana," my father declares, his mouth full of bread. "That doesn't have any pork, right?"

"Excuse me?" Asher asks.

"You know, pork," my father says. This night is starting to feel surreal. My father and Asher Richelli are talking about pork! "We don't eat anything from a pig," my father explains. "We're Muslim."

I swear, it would be so much easier if whenever my family went out to eat we wore T-shirts that said "No Booze! No Pork! (We're Muslim)" in big letters across the front.

"No, there's no pork. It's just veal, you know, *veal* parmigiana." Asher smiles weakly, like he's not sure if his joke is funny or not. He pronounces *veal parmigiana* in his Italian accent, and it makes my heart pang.

"But we always like to check," my mother explains. "Sometimes restaurants put pork in their dishes even though it doesn't mention it on the menu."

"Oh, I understand. I'm half-Jewish," Asher says. "Anything else?"

"No," I tell him. "Thank you."

We watch Asher walk away in silence, then my mother says, "Half-Jewish? I bet he's smart. Is he in your year?" What she means is, Will he be competing with you to get into Yale?

"No," I lie.

The restaurant fills up and Asher has a bunch of other tables to wait on, so the busboy brings us our entrees. "My *biryani* is so much better than this. We could have stayed home and eaten that," my mother states, though this doesn't prevent her from finishing off her entire entree. My father cleans his plate within ten minutes. I mostly pick at mine.

"Why aren't you eating?" my father asks.

"I'm not that hungry," I say.

He reaches his hand across the table. "Give it to me, I'll eat it."

"Jamshed!" My mother grabs his wrist. "Think of your choles-terol!" My father rolls his eyes at me, but returns his hand to his lap.

When Asher comes over to ask us if we want any dessert, my father opens his mouth to say yes but my mother raises her eyebrows at him so he shakes his head no instead. "Can you pack this?" she asks Asher, pointing at my entree.

"Of course," Asher says, taking my plate.

Then she points to the half-eaten loaf of bread that's still sitting in the basket. "Pack that too," she tells Asher.

"Sure thing." Asher is smiling now, and I'm positive he's trying not to laugh.

When he comes back with our bill and the doggie bag he pauses after he puts them down. "Did you enjoy your meal?" he asks.

"Yes, it was perfecto!" my father exclaims, pronouncing *perfecto* in an exaggerated Italian accent.

"Excellent," Asher says. I expect him to leave us now but he stays, fingering the edge of the tablecloth. "I know Nina has to study really hard and everything, but it'd be nice if we got to see more of her outside of school too. I'm sure you know you have a really great daughter."

What on earth has gotten into Asher's head? "Thank you," my father says as Asher walks away, oblivious to the tension his comment has created.

"What did he mean by that?" my mother asks.

This night has gone from surreal to plain bad. "I guess people think it's strange they don't see me much on weekends," I say.

"Are you sure that he's not interested in you?" my mother hisses. "He isn't that Robbie boy, is he?"

I laugh. "Ma, I told you his name is Asher. He's one of the most popular guys in school. Trust me, he doesn't like me. He feels sorry for me."

My mother's eyes widen. "Why should he feel sorry for you?" she demands. "There's nothing to feel sorry about."

It's enough to make me want to drown myself in a sea of Alfredo sauce. "No, of course there isn't," I say. I check the bill to make sure my father left a good tip. Asher is nowhere to be seen, and it's the perfect time to make a quick exit. "Let's go."

As we walk through the restaurant, my mother stops suddenly. "Nina," she whispers. "Isn't that Bridget?"

I follow the direction of her eyes. Sure enough, there are Bridget and Anthony sitting at a table in the corner, fingers entwined over a flickering candle flame. Neither of them sees us. This night has now officially gone from surreal to bad to much, much worse. How can I talk myself out of this one?

"Come on!" I say, pushing my mother forward, past the Leaning Tower of Pisa and fake potted plants, ignoring the hostess as she waves goodbye.

Color-Blind

When we get in the car my mother swivels around and looks at me. "Bridget is dating a black boy?"

I'm not sure what to do. Denial is not an option, considering what she just saw, so I decide to play dumb. "I don't know."

"Of course you know! Bridget is your friend." She's cupped her hand over her mouth in dismay and is talking through her fingers. "Do her parents know?"

"Of course they know, Farzana." I can tell by my father's tone of voice that he's about to enter sarcastic mode like he always does when he gets worked up about the lack of morality in Western culture. "American parents don't mind if their teenage daughters go on dates with boys. It makes them happy. Bridget's parents probably threw a party when they found out."

"But with a black boy?" my mother says.

"Who cares if he's black?" I retort.

"It's not that he's black, it's that . . ." She pauses.

"That he's black," I say. "You guys look down on black people. Admit it." My motives here are twofold: to confront my parents about their own racism, and to distract them from the topic of my friends' love lives.

"That's not true. Some are very smart and hardworking, like the nurses at the hospital, and Mr. Hutchinson and his family," my mother protests.

"Would you say that about white people?" I ask.

"I would say it about everyone. Some white people are lazy, some are hardworking. Same with Pakistanis. But don't change the subject." She looks me straight in the eye, as if this will make for a more fruitful inquisition. "Does Helena have a boyfriend too?" she asks, but doesn't wait for my response. "I am sure she does. If Bridget has one, then Helena probably does too, right?"

"Come on," I protest. "What's the big deal? They're my oldest friends, and just because I hang out with them doesn't mean I'm going to start doing the things they do."

"Nina, I have known Helena and Bridget for many years. I know they are nice girls. But some things that are okay for them are wrong for you. If you spend too much time with them you may want to go to dinner with boys too." My mother presses her lips together so hard they turn a pale pinkish white. "I don't think you should go to Helena's house tomorrow night. There are going to be boys there, right?"

"I told you it's only girls!" I yell.

"If you want to have them come over to our house, that's fine," my mother says. "But you shouldn't be staying at their houses so late at night."

"I'll come home earlier. Dad can pick me up at eleven instead of one," I offer.

"We are doing this for your own good," my mother says. "One day you will have children and understand. End of discussion."

I push my knees against the back of the seat. As Allah is my witness, when I have my own children, I will allow them to attend every sleepover their hearts desire.

After we pull into the driveway my father shuts off the car, but instead of opening the door he looks at me. "Muhammad Ali is black," he says. "And a good Muslim." He takes his index finger and points it at his eyes. "Allah, you see, is color-blind."

Superlative Afternoons

How was the sleepover?" I ask Helena on Monday on our way to the cafeteria.

"It was lovely. The witch baked us delicious cookies and showed us how to tape our boobs in the unlikely event that one of us decides to sign up for a beauty pageant. Serena came in your place. We really missed you." She takes my arm. "More importantly, how are you doing? Are your parents still upset?"

I shake my head. "Well, considering I'd always acted like you and Bridget were nuns, they felt like I hadn't been honest with them, but they still think you're nice girls."

"Who's a nice girl?" Bridget says, walking up to us.

"We are, apparently," Helena replies. "Will you still be able to do things with us?"

"Well, I think nocturnal activities will have to be approved on an individual basis and only after a thorough interrogation. But my mom must feel a little bad, because last night she came into my room and told me I could sleep over at Asiya's or Saba's whenever I wanted. Anyway, let's talk about something else. Bridget, how did your big night go?"

Bridget sticks her tongue into one side of her cheek, makes a popping sound, and winks at me.

"Bridget!" Helena cries.

"Do you want to hear the gory details?" Bridget asks.

I wouldn't mind, but Helena claps her hands over her ears, and then Bridget says, "Ahoy! Nina's man is heading our way."

In the span of a few seconds, my friends have abandoned my side and Asher has taken their place. "Hey, Nina," he says. "Listen, I realized last night that maybe what I said to your parents wasn't the smartest thing. I hope I didn't get you into trouble or anything."

Oh, my thoughtful, sweet darling! Oh, my sun-kissed Mediterranean Adonis! "Don't worry about it. I know you meant well. But my parents aren't going to change that easily, and definitely not on the suggestion of some boy they don't even know."

Asher nods. His forehead starts to crinkle, and my heart starts to melt. "I'm really sorry, Nina," he apologizes. "I was just trying to help."

"It's fine, really," I tell him. "They weren't upset."

"Did your parents enjoy the food, at least?" he asks.

Before I can answer, Laura McNutt steps between Asher and me. I didn't even see her coming, but here she is, in a red-and-white-striped sweater and white pants and red earrings, like a skulking candy cane. "What's up?" she says, elbowing Asher and not even acknowledging me. "Have you recovered from Cassie's party yet?"

Asher smiles. "Barely," he says. "You guys know each other, right?"

Laura nods at me. "Yeah, I know Nina. How've you been?"

"Good. I gotta go." As I leave, my backpack falls off my shoulder and I grab it and head inside the cafeteria, trying not to imagine how dorky I must look in my jeans and turtleneck sweater, cradling a backpack to my chest. I swear I can hear Laura McNutt snickering.

Bridget has requested a girls-only lunch so she can relay the details of her romantic night, but I can't seem to pay attention. "Why so glum, plum?" Bridget asks. It takes me a second to realize she's addressing me. She and Anthony are beginning to sound more and more alike.

"Do you think I should make like Laura McButt and throw myself at Asher?"

"Of course not," Helena says. "That's so gauche."

"I wish I could snap my fingers and make him fall for me." I put my head on the table and Helena starts rubbing my back.

"I wish I could help out somehow," she says.

"It couldn't hurt for you to flirt with him more," Bridget says. "Every time you talk to him you look a little constipated."

"You know, Bridget, there is a time for humor and there is a time for empathy and one day you should really learn the difference," Helena tells her.

I decide to take off before their bickering begins. Biology is the last class of the day and by the time it rolls around I am exhausted and cranky and have to perform day two of frog dissection. Helena is usually my lab partner, but she got excused from dissection because she thinks it's cruel and the sight of guts makes her nauseated, so I have to remove and unravel a long intestine by myself, which seems like a fitting end to a crappy afternoon. When I leave biology Asher is waiting for me. I know he's waiting for me because as soon as I walk out of the classroom he says my name, and I'm surprised because I didn't realize he knew my class schedule, even though I have his memorized.

"I thought I could give you a ride home," he says.

"I smell like formaldehyde," I tell him.

He smiles one of his lopsided smiles. "You smell fine. Look, I know a ride home won't make up for my stupidity, but it would make me feel better."

I'm about to refuse and remind him that me accepting a ride home from a boy would be a bad idea, but then I think about how everyone in this entire school must be experiencing new things and taking risks, and why can't I take one small risk for once in my life? "Sure,"

I say. "But you'll have to drop me off a few blocks away from my house."

The two of us walk out of school and into the parking lot together and I'm secretly hoping that every girl in Deer Hook High is watching me right now, rubbing her eyes in disbelief. Half of me is nervous and the other half feels like shouting triumphantly, "Yes, the girl walking away with Asher is, indeed, Nina Khan. Eat your heart out, Deer Hook High."

Asher's car is an old, dark red Toyota Celica. Scattered across the backseat are a couple of notebooks, a copy of *Romeo and Juliet*, and athletic gear: two pairs of sneakers and gym clothes and a basketball and an empty Gatorade bottle.

"Sorry," Asher says. "I haven't had a chance to clean up."

"That's all right."

"Maybe I should air out the car for a second." Asher rolls down his window, and I hope it's not because I smell like formaldehyde. As he leans past me to roll down mine, his lovely waves of hair are so close that if I move forward just an inch I could bury my face in them.

"How much longer till you get your license?" he asks, returning to his seat.

"I actually have my test this week," I say. He starts the car and then he leans over again to roll up my window, his head so near my chest that I'm sure he can hear my heart pounding.

"That's great!" He sounds more enthusiastic than I feel. "It's an awesome feeling to get your license. People start to take you more seriously, probably because you're more useful to them."

"I know, I can't wait."

Asher turns onto Main Street and we drive by the pizza place. I see Mr. Weber, the owner, inside, and panic. Mr. Weber is one of my father's patients, as are numerous other people in Deer Hook. A lot of people in Deer Hook know my parents are Muslim and conservative. What if one of them sees me and later tells my father, "I saw your daughter driving around Deer Hook with a handsome fella"? How could I be so stupid? I have no choice; I sink way down in my seat.

"Nina? What are you doing?" Asher asks.

I look up at him. "I can't let anyone see me in the car with you. What if one of my dad's patients sees me and tells my parents?" I explain. "I'm so dumb. I should have thought of this before."

Asher shakes his head. "I can't believe this. I'm getting you into trouble again."

"No, you were just being nice. Anyway, this is kind of fun."

Asher laughs. "You're crazy, you know that?"

"I'll take that as a compliment," I say. "Where are we now?"

"We just turned onto Burnett. Where do you want me to drop you off?"

"At the corner of Maple and Burnett. By the way, I really liked the food at your restaurant."

"My mother will be happy to hear that—she supervises all the cooks. So we're here," he says, slowing down. "You want me to make sure there's no one around?"

"Please."

He does a quick survey, then makes a fist and talks into it. "This is Asher to base, Asher to base. The coast is clear. I repeat, the coast is clear."

I'm laughing so hard when I tell him thanks and goodbye I'm not even sure he understands what I said. After I get out I'm too scared to look back, then Asher drives away, and I wonder if he is looking at me in his rearview mirror. This is the most fun I've had in ages. Who knew this day would go from crappy to superlative? I wouldn't mind if all my days began badly if only they ended like this.

Allah's Gift to the Earth

When I get home I head straight to my room and two seconds later there's a knock on my door. It's my mother. Of course the day I decide to accept a ride home from a boy couldn't be one of the days she works late at the office. I'm never lucky like that.

"Where were you walking home from?" she asks.

My heart is now racing for a different reason. It's amazing how fine a line there is between exhilaration and fear. But before I can determine the best response, I need more clarification. "What do you mean?"

"I saw you walking down the street. Where were you coming from?"

"Oh, Helena dropped me off," I reply.

"But why didn't she drop you off in front of the house?"

Think, Nina, think. "Because she forgot something important at school and had to go back and get it before she got locked out."

"Really?" my mother says. She's almost bought it. "What did she forget?"

"Her biology textbook. We have a quiz tomorrow."

"Oh." My mother nods. Sold! "Well, you're getting your license this week so you won't have to take rides from your friends." She hesitates and drums her fingers against my door frame. "You didn't mention to Bridget that we saw her at that restaurant, did you?"

I know my mother doesn't like me to talk about what goes on in our family with "outsiders," so I tell her no.

"Good. There's no need for her to know," she reminds me. "Oh, and we have to go to a wedding tomorrow. Guess who's getting married?"

"Who?"

"Huma."

Huma! I'm surprised my mother is being so blasé about Huma marrying a white boy. "Wow, that's really great," I say. And it is. Maybe at the wedding my mother will be so emotionally touched by the love between Huma and Ian, she'll become more open to me marrying a white boy. Stranger things have happened, right?

"She's marrying a boy named Kashif," my mother continues.

"Kashif? Who's that? And didn't this wedding thing happen a little fast?"

"Sometimes, if you find such a nice boy, it's better to move quickly. He's getting an MBA from Columbia and he's from a wealthy industrialist family from Lahore. What a catch! If I were to present such a boy to Sonia, I'm sure she would find some reason to reject him!" she exclaims, scowling at me as if this were my fault. The subject of marriage seems to rile my mother up more and more each week. I'm glad I'm the youngest and won't have to deal with this whole marriage business for a while, but right now there's no one else for her to take her frustration out on besides me. "You kids are too stubborn! You think you deserve some kind of prince. Let me ask you, what makes you so special? Do you think you are Allah's gift to the earth?"

"Ma, I can assure you I don't think I am Allah's gift to the earth. And if I was, I hope for the world's sake I came with a return receipt."

My mother frowns. "There is nothing funny about this. You have to help me with your sister. She needs to start taking marriage seriously. Maybe you should talk to her."

"Ma, Sonia and I don't talk like that," I say.

"Why aren't you close with your sister?" she asks, jabbing her finger at me when she says "you," because apparently this is my fault as well.

"Why don't you ask her that? She's the one who's never here!"

My mother grips the door frame like she's worried she can't support her own weight. "In Pakistan, families are so close. Of course people fight, but everyone lives together, grows up together. Here, you don't even know where your kids are. Here, your own daughter hangs up the phone on you!" I don't know what she's referencing, but I assume she must have had a fight with Sonia and is exaggerating the outcome, because I can't imagine Sonia hanging up on her. "Huma is only one year older than Sonia, but she is a nice girl who listens to her mother." As I think of an appropriate response that will make my mother feel better while still being supportive of my sister, my mother says, "Don't worry, get back to your studies," and makes an abrupt departure.

And now, instead of reliving each delicious moment of my ride with Asher, I'm thinking about Huma's impending wedding. I wonder if she ever told her mother about Ian, and how Ian feels about her marrying someone else. If her parents would have accepted Ian, would she still have broken up with him? Does she love this guy Kashif? Does she regret having a secret relationship, or is she happy she got to know Ian? How can you know when the risks of something will outweigh the rewards, or vice versa?

The Whore from Lahore

My mother claims that Huma's wedding is on a Tuesday because Huma's father is really cheap and got a 50 percent discount by having it so early in the week. By the time we arrive, there are already hundreds of people milling around the banquet hall, the women in formal Pakistani attire that encompasses every variation of every color known to man. I'm wearing a light pink *gharara*, which sort of looks like a skirt but is really pants that flare out from the knee. "It's what the Mughal princesses used to wear," my mother tells me, but I feel oafish in it. I have three-inch heels on and every time I take a step I worry that I will trip over my *gharara* and fall flat on my face. I'm also wearing pink and gold glass bangles on both of my arms. For some reason they never make these bangles for girls with thick wrists like mine, and in spite of my hands and arms being slathered in soap and my mother sliding the bracelets on carefully as she pressed the fleshy part of my thumb against my palm, a bunch of them still broke. I've got tiny gashes from the broken glass on my arms, which are hidden by the bangles that managed to survive. I don't understand why everything that's supposed to make you beautiful has to hurt so much.

At the end of the banquet hall are two gold thronelike chairs. Huma is sitting in one of them. She's dressed in a *gharara* also, except she really does look like a princess. Her hands are decorated with henna and she's wearing intricate gold jewelry and a large gold hoop through her nose and lots of makeup and a heavily embroidered deep red *dupatta* is pinned to her head. She looks beautiful, but so fragile, like she might break under the pressure of it all. Next to her is her husband, Kashif, who's wearing a turban and a traditional *sherwani*, which is sort of like a slim-fitting coat that ends at the knees, and polished black shoes that stand out against his starched white clothes. His score on the prestige points scale must be high, since he's tall and fair and getting his MBA. People keep coming on and off the stage to congratulate and take pictures with the couple and since I've been here Huma hasn't looked up or smiled. She's opted for the suicide-bride demeanor, but whether it's because she feels like she ought to or because she actually feels sad I can't tell.

The rest of the room is crowded with round tables draped with red tablecloths and at one end the caterers are busy setting up for the buffet dinner and there's a bar where you can get soda and mango punch, which is where most of the uncles have converged.

"Hi, Nina." It's Asiya. She's standing by herself in a gold sari. She has almost as much makeup on as Huma and looks great, like some lost Bollywood heroine who wandered onto the wrong movie set.

"Asiya! You look so nice!" my mother says.

"Thanks, Auntie," Asiya answers, adjusting the *pallu* of her sari. After a girl reaches a certain age, weddings aren't just weddings, they're an opportunity for her to be on display for the aunties who may have a son or nephew who would be a good catch, as well as for all of the single male friends and relatives of the groom who might be present.

"Let's go congratulate the bride and groom," my mother tells me, and we start weaving our way through the tables. I shadow my mother, nodding *salaams* to the people onstage. We wait in line to greet the bride and groom, and when it's our turn my mother grasps Huma's hands between her own and exclaims in Urdu, "Huma! I remember when you were a little girl playing hide-and-seek with Sonia. Congratulations! I hope Allah gives you a long, happy marriage." Huma lifts her eyes for a second and says thank you quietly. Then she sees me. "Hi, Nina," she says, even more quietly.

"Congratulations," I say, and Huma's eyes, which are lined with thick black eyeliner, are so bright and moist that for a second I'm scared she might cry.

Kashif's turban is too big and is falling down his forehead. My mother introduces herself and me and adjusts his turban for him. He smiles and he has a gap between his teeth like Asher, except it's on the bottom. "Nice to meet you," he says. I'm probably the eight-millionth person he's had to meet tonight and I'm sure he won't remember me. It seems really tedious, to have to engage in social pleasantries with so many people, a lot of whom you don't even know, but Kashif seems thrilled, probably because he's won the jackpot in the pretty wives' lottery.

After we leave my mother says, "She is such a good girl it breaks my heart," placing her hand over her heart as if it's a literal statement.

"Farzana!" It's Yasmin Auntie, Huma's mother. She holds my mother's arm above the elbow and pumps it a little bit. She looks more excited than I've ever seen her. "So glad you are here!"

"She is such a beautiful bride," my mother says.

"One day Sonia will be a beautiful bride too," Yasmin Auntie offers. My mother is silent. "And so will you, Nina, eh?" Yasmin Auntie continues. "Come, Nina, why don't you meet Kashif's cousin?" She takes my hand and leads me to one of the tables near the front, where a young woman is sitting. She's also wearing a gold sari, like Asiya, but she looks like she could be a bona fide model, tall and skinny with shining ebony locks. "Nina, this is Zainab. She is Kashif's cousin from Lahore. She is studying at a college in New York City." Great—as if I needed this juxtaposition; me, the oaf in a *gharara*, next to someone who looks like she just stepped off a runway.

"Hello," Zainab says, in a slightly British Pakistani accent.

Yasmin Auntie has disappeared. I don't know what to do, so I sit down next to Zainab, leaving one chair between us. "Hello."

"Are you related to Huma?" Zainab asks.

"I grew up with her. Well, my sister did more than me." I look down at my feet. I'm wearing open-toed shoes with stockings, which Maria once told Helena is a major fashion *don't*. My toes are painted with pink nail polish from my mother's drawer that's almost the exact shade of my outfit, and half of it has come off my left big toe.

Zainab turns toward me and her gleaming mane of hair swings back, shampoo-commercial-style. "Why does the actual wedding have to be so boring? At least at the *mehndi* event there's dancing and *hungama*." *Hungama* can mean a few different things but in this context it means raucousness, like people dancing and having fun everywhere. She has a point; the *mehndi* event, where women put on henna and sing and girls and guys perform dances, is considerably more fun than any of the other wedding functions.

"It wouldn't really be a Pakistani event if it wasn't kind of boring," I tell her. "I mean, most of them are pretty much the same. The aunties gossip, the uncles talk about politics, everyone eats a lot, and then it's over."

Zainab looks at me quizzically. She has thick eyelashes and dramatic cheekbones. I try not to stare at her, but she's just too striking. If I looked like this, would Asher fall for me? "Have you ever been to any parties in Pakistan?" she asks.

"I've never been to Pakistan. I'm going for the first time over Christmas break."

"You should come visit Lahore, then. You'd have a blast," she says, and I must look doubtful, because she adds, "You don't think so?"

"It's just that Pakistan seems to be a million more times likely to have a blast than to be a blast," I say. Zainab does not look amused and I wish I could take back my joke.

"Is that really what you think of Pakistan?" she asks.

"Well, according to my mother, it's a great place to raise children because they'll grow up with a thorough knowledge of Islam and have strong ties to their family and listen to their parents."

Zainab runs the tip of her finger along the edge of her punch glass. "Well, that is true for some people. But it's not quite as simple as that. There are a lot of people in Pakistan who drink and engage in other so-called un-Islamic activities."

"No way." I can't imagine Nasreen Khala rubbing shoulders with anyone who engaged in un-Islamic activities.

"It's true. Some of the teenagers there have boyfriends and drink and go to parties, all the things teenagers do over here, but over there, it happens behind closed doors, more or less. Personally, I don't do those things, but if that's the kind of fun you're looking for, you can have a lot of it there too, if you know the right people."

"But I don't understand. Don't they get into trouble?" I ask her. It's hard for me to reconcile this Pakistan, where certain teenagers may engage in more acts of rebellion than I do, apparently with much more ease, with my mother's Pakistan, where the call to prayer was always met with obedient, God-fearing ears.

Zainab puts her hand up. "Don't misunderstand, of course it's a Muslim country, and girls there are concerned with their reputation. Sleep with one boy too many and you might be known as the whore of Lahore." I'm surprised that she's being so frank with me, but it's cool because it means she thinks I'm somebody worthy of her frankness. "And it's mostly the upper class that has these kinds of parties. But the image of Pakistan your mother has in her head is a relic from 1970. It's the 1990s now, and we have bearded mullahs giving impassioned speeches about Islamic piety while girls wearing skimpy dresses dance the night away under guava trees, and everything in between. And there are so many other things that are fun, like the shopping, and the poetry, and the music. Have you ever been to an all-night *qawwali* show?"

"No, but I think I've heard my father sing every *qawwali* song that has ever existed," I say.

She smiles. "Well, when they go back your parents will see how Pakistan has changed and how it hasn't. It really is a fascinating place."

I'm already fascinated, and I want to ask her more questions, but some auntie I don't recognize comes over and tells Zainab to come for pictures. Zainab follows her, walking elegantly in her sparkling sari, and takes her place behind the thrones with other people I don't recognize, who must be the groom's family.

"Look at her sari."

I look up. Asiya is standing behind me. "She's the groom's cousin," I tell her. "She's from Lahore."

"I know who she is," Asiya says. "That sari is so beautiful. It makes mine look frumpy."

She's right. Zainab's sari is by far the most stunning one here. "Yours is really beautiful too."

"You think so?" Asiya says.

"I'm the one that looks frumpy. It's impossible for me to look elegant in a *gharara*," I say.

"That's okay." Asiya sits down. "No one's looking at you."

Saba walks over to us, two mango punches in her hand. "You should see how much mango punch the uncles are drinking. Someone should go spike it with something. Then this party would really get going!"

Asiya takes a sip of the punch, her eyes on the bride. "Poor Huma," she says. "She's been through a tough time. I feel like any minute now she might burst into tears."

I can't contain my curiosity any longer. "Asiya? What happened between Huma and that guy Ian?"

Asiya leans toward me, but doesn't lower her voice. "She knew that if she married Ian it would break her parents' hearts, and she wouldn't be happy if they weren't happy, so she broke up with Ian. He said he'd convert and everything, but she told him it wouldn't be the same. And one month later her parents introduced her to Kashif, and about two seconds later they got engaged."

"But she likes this Kashif guy, right?"

Asiya shrugs. "She told me she does, but who knows?"

"She looks so pretty," Saba says. "Her eyes remind me of a mermaid, you know, sitting on a rock, hoping for someone to come and make her human."

"Well, I hope this guy's that someone," Asiya says. "I heard Kashif is kind of spoiled. I was supposed to be introduced to him, but his mother thought I was too young. Now I'm glad everything worked out the way it did."

"Who is that woman talking to Huma?" Saba asks. "She looks like a model."

Asiya speaks before I can answer. "That's Kashif's cousin. Apparently their family is one of the richest in Lahore. And you know how it is over there—if you're rich, you rule the world, at least that world."

I don't know how it is over there, but looking at Zainab it doesn't take much to imagine her walking down some red carpet in Lahore, smiling coyly at the photographers she rules over. Suddenly masses of people start moving in the same direction, which can mean only one thing—dinner is being served.

"Thank God," Saba says. "I'm starving."

We stand up, but Asiya stays seated. "I'm not hungry," she tells us.

"Bitter, anyone?" Saba whispers to me as we head toward the buffet. I don't respond. After all, I'm no stranger to jealousy. I've been jealous of a certain blond girl, and, once in a while, I've even been jealous of my own friends.

"When do you think your sister will get married?" Saba asks.

I try to picture Sonia in a red *gharara* with dark eye shadow on her lids. I don't think I've ever seen Sonia wearing eye shadow. She'd probably bring a book to her own wedding in case she got bored and needed intellectual stimulation. "I don't think she's getting married anytime soon."

"Good," Saba says. "The more girls in our community who marry later, the better it is for us."

Although I'm sure altruism isn't one of the reasons Sonia's not interested in marriage, Saba does have a point.

I wait for the inevitable on the ride home. First my parents perform their obligatory critique of the various dishes served and discussion of who said what about whom, and then my mother sighs. "Huma's mother is so lucky. What are we going to do about Sonia? Whenever I bring up marriage, she stops talking to me."

"Don't worry," my father says. "Sonia will find a nice boy to marry. She's young, she has lots of time."

"But the good boys are so hard to find," my mother replies. "Do you think Sonia will find a nice boy one day?" It takes a second for me to realize that my mother is asking me this. I decide to piggyback on my father's confidence.

"Yeah, definitely," I say.

She relaxes her head against the seat. "Yes," she says, nodding. "I think so too."

Do You Want to Ride in My Mercedes, Boy?

The next day, I achieve a milestone that's truly worthy of celebration—I get my driver's license.

"Guess who got a license to drive this morning?" I announce at lunch.

"That's wonderful! You're an independent woman now," Helena says, clapping.

"That depends on your definition of independence," I reply.

"Finally," Anthony says. "Girl's got wheels."

"Yeah, I've got my sister's crappy old car that she practically totaled once," I gripe.

"Better than no car," Bridget points out. "But it's too bad that now Asher won't be able to give you rides home."

"Nina's going to be giving Asher rides home," Anthony says, and Bridget giggles like it's some kind of dirty joke.

"Nina! You have to ask him like this," Bridget explains, and she waves her arms in front of her and sings, " 'Do you wanna ride in my Mercedes,' Asherrr?"

" 'Tell me what you gonna do with me,' " Anthony continues, and now they're both laughing so hard they're holding their stomachs.

"The two of you should really star together in a Bollywood movie," I tell them.

"What's a Bollywood movie?" Anthony asks.

"These Indian movies where everyone dances and sings," Bridget explains. "I saw part of one at Nina's house when I was little.

157

Some man and woman were singing and going down a hill on roller skates."

"That's from *Seeta aur Geeta*!" I say. "You remember that?"

"We could sing a song going downhill on skis," Bridget tells Anthony.

"First you have to get me on them," Anthony says. "You'd have better luck waiting for the devil to put a snow cone machine in hell."

"That's my line!" Bridget snaps. She turns to us. "Anthony says he won't ski because he doesn't like the cold, but it's really because he's scared of heights."

Anthony's face fattens—when he's annoyed he puffs out his cheeks like Sonia does. "Did you have to tell them that?"

"That's why we call her Big Mouth Bridget," I inform him, but Anthony doesn't hear me because he's too busy arguing with Bridget.

"I need to powder my nose," Helena says.

"Me too," I say. I follow Helena through the cafeteria and down the hall to the girls' bathroom next to the teachers' lounge. Helena is quiet at first, examining her face in the mirror.

"So I broke up with Vinny," she confesses.

"You did? How did it go?"

"He cried, and then he said he knew all along that I was too good for him. Of course I told him right away that wasn't true. I really tried to fall in love with him, I did." Now she looks like she's about to cry. "But it takes more than will to fall in love with someone. I just couldn't do it. Why can't dating be easy? Why can't it ever be girl meets boy and they live happily ever after?"

"Well, they may be arguing right now, but Bridget and Anthony seem pretty happy," I say.

"They do, don't they?" Helena splashes some water on her face. "Anyway! How is everything going with Asher?"

"There's no everything," I say. "There was just that one thing, and since our ride together we haven't even talked that much. I don't know. For a second, in his car, I really thought it was possible that he might like me, but now I'm pretty sure he thinks of me as some girl he likes to pal around with once in a while."

"Have you thought about what you would do if Asher came up to you and told you he liked you?"

"Like that's going to happen."

"But it could," Helena insists. "Would you date him?"

"You know I can't date."

"But you could eat lunch together in school every day—isn't that kind of dating?"

"Yeah. Lame dating."

"You wouldn't try to have any kind of relationship with him at all?"

"It's complicated. What would you do if you were in my situation?"

"I don't know," she says. "On the one hand, how can you not explore an opportunity for love? But then I'd feel so guilty whenever I saw my father, and we're so young, we'll have lots of time to explore love, right? You know, last time I saw my mother she was telling me how she was too young when she married my father and if she had waited maybe things between them would have turned out differently. Then she said, 'Helena Sophia, if you only ever heed one piece of advice from me, heed this—never underestimate the importance of timing.' "

"It's so nice you can have talks like that with your mother," I tell her.

"I'd rather see her every day like you see yours." I wish I knew the right thing to say whenever Helena laments her mother's absence, something that would make her laugh and feel better and forget about the ache in her heart, but the best I can offer is an ear and a hug. "Anyway," she continues, "I guess you can cross that bridge when you come to it."

I nod. "But just because I don't know if Asher and I could have a real future together doesn't mean I'd mind kissing him."

Helena laughs. "Who wouldn't?"

Within seconds of leaving the bathroom we run into the man himself, and Helena mumbles some excuse and heads back to the cafeteria.

"Hey, Nina." Ah, that voice, the way he inflects his greeting—Hey, *Ni*-na. I could listen to it on repeat all day. "Did you pass your driving test yet?"

I nod and Asher raises his hand for a high-five and I raise mine and I don't know how, but I completely miss it and end up high-fiving the air above his left shoulder.

Asher laughs. "Don't worry, you don't need much hand-eye coordination to drive," he quips, winking. And there's the *keera* in my brain again, whispering, "Ask not for whom those long eyelashes wink, they wink for . . ." Shut up!

"Did you say something?" Asher asks.

"Sorry," I say. "I was talking to myself."

He grins. "I knew you were crazy," he says over his shoulder as he walks away.

If I could write the script of my own life, here is how it would go: Yes, Asher, I am crazy, crazy in love with you, I'd tell him. Hey, Nina, he'd reply, why didn't you tell me before? Because I'm crazy about you too. And then he'd repeat the word *crazy*, but in Italian this time, and cut to the next scene, where it's Italian countryside and tiramisu and *bellissima, bellissima, bellissima*.

College Boys and Soggy Bread

This is it, the end of the first half of junior year. Winter formal is this weekend. Everyone is annoyed that it's happening so close to exams, but that's not going to stop anyone from getting wasted and staying up the entire night, at least according to Bridget. "I am going to get so plastered," she tells us. We got to school early today to help sort the toys our school received from its annual holiday toy drive. We still have half an hour before school officially begins and Helena and I are cramming for our French final while Bridget files her nails, something she never used to do before dating Anthony. "I almost forgot!" Bridget says. "I heard Laura McButt asked Asher to formal and he said no."

"Who is he going with?" I ask.

"Apparently he's not going. What do you think of that piece of news?"

"I can't pretend that it doesn't please me immensely."

Helena blurts out, "Shannon Kelly asked me if I would ask him to go to formal with me. And so I did."

"But you don't even like him," I say. "I thought that after Vinny, you were only going to go out with boys you really like."

"I know," she says. "But I made it clear that we were only going as friends."

Bridget laughs. "He must have peed his pants when you asked him. I think he's been wanting to go out with you since he was in the womb."

"We're not going out," Helena protests. "We're just going to formal together. As friends."

"You think he's not going to try to get in your pants?" Bridget asks.

"Certainly not!" Helena exclaims. "Anyway, I'm wearing a dress. So why do you think Asher isn't going to formal?" She directs this question at me, as if I have a psychic link to his brain.

"Because he decided he'd only go if he could go with me, obviously." I skipped breakfast this morning and start unwrapping the tuna sandwich I brought for lunch. The bread is already soggy. "You know what? My New Year's resolution is going to be to stop obsessing over Asher and do more productive things with my time."

"Like SAT practice exams?" Bridget says.

Before I can think of a witty retort, Serena walks up to us, her hair pulled back in a perfect French braid. Bridget told me her mother does this for her and Serena makes her do it over if it's not exactly right. Her cardigan is unzipped and underneath she's wearing a tight green tank top that says "I ♥ Deer Hook Game Farm."

"Hey, guys," she says, sitting next to us. "Did you see all the stuffed animals my parents donated from the game farm gift shop? They are so adorable. I wanted to steal one for myself, but I already have, like, twenty of them." Then she starts smiling so widely her button nose looks like someone inflated it

"What are you so happy about?" Bridget asks.

"I'm in love," she tells us.

"That's wonderful! Who's the lucky boy?" Helena asks.

"His name is Rory, and he is the most amazing boy I've ever met." Serena hugs herself. "He goes to college and he's interning at the game farm and he wants to be a veterinarian."

"A college boy! Nice," Bridget says.

Helena nods. "Older men is the way to go. High school boys are so juvenile."

"Tell me about it. Anyway, I want him to come to formal but he says he's too old, so instead we might go to New York City for the weekend."

"Your parents would let you go to New York City with some guy in college?" Bridget asks.

"Of course. They adore Rory," Serena says. "Not everyone's parents are like Nina's, right?"

I don't honor this with a reply.

"Don't worry," she tells me. "One day you'll meet a wonderful boy too. Maybe not here, but there'll be so many more boys in college."

"I wasn't worried," I reply. Silence.

"Well, I have to go." Serena stands up. "I really want you guys to meet Rory sometime. I was thinking of having a bunch of people over for dinner at my house around New Year's, you know, like a proper dinner party."

"Sounds like fun," Bridget says.

"She really does look happy," Helena says after Serena leaves.

"What the hell did she mean?" I ask. "I'll be able to meet someone in college because the more boys there are, the higher my statistical chance of one of them actually liking me?"

"Nina, she was only trying to be nice," Helena says.

"If that's her definition of nice, what is her definition of mean? Taking an ax and actually stabbing me in the back with it?"

"Don't you think you're overreacting a little?" Bridget says.

Bridget and Helena are never 100 percent on my side on the Serena issue, like I want them to be. I squeeze my sandwich into a ball and toss it at the garbage can. I miss by at least a foot, but I leave it on the floor and stomp away. That was a dumb thing to do, because I feel guilty for littering and now I have to go wash the tuna fish smell from my hands.

A Match Made in Heaven

Mr. Porcupine passes out a problem set. "I was going to hand this out as something you could do on your own to prepare for the final, but I've decided to have you do it in pairs instead, so you can help and learn from one another."

Ricca raises her hand. "But we never do anything in pairs," she says, even though she does everything in a pair with Cassie Banks.

"There are seven problems," Mr. Porcupine continues, "and you'll be graded on your answers." He pauses, waiting for the collective class groan to end. "It's due the day of our exam, which, in case any of you forgot, is on Monday. I've already divided you up." He starts to read from a list on his desk. "Simon Yearling and Tricia Haines."

My hands are closed tight around the edges of my desk as I recite in my head, Please let it be Asher, only him only him. If there is an Allah in heaven, if there is an Allah in heaven . . . "Ricca Rimes and David Margolis. Nina Khan and Asher Richelli." There is an Allah in heaven!

"So, when do you want to do this?" Asher asks me after class.

"Sunday afternoon?" I suggest.

"That's fine with me. Should we meet at the library?"

I can't allow us to meet somewhere as unromantic as the public library. "I can come over to your house."

"You can?" He looks surprised. "That's cool with me if it's cool with you. My house is the last one at the dead end of Locust Grove Road."

"Three o'clock?" I ask.

He nods. "See you then."

"Have fun at formal," I say, even though I know he's not going.

"Can't go. There's a wedding reception at the restaurant tomorrow night and I've got to work. But you have fun."

"I'm not going either."

"Oh, right. Sorry, I forgot you're—"

"Don't worry about it," I say and walk away, counting my steps. When I hit five I do a half-turn and give him a little wave. He smiles, and I continue my walk, cool as the cucumbers my mother chops up for her yogurt *raita*. Could I have played that scene any better? I think not.

Playbreaker

I spend Saturday studying, drinking lots of hot chocolate with marshmallows, and trying not to think too much about my "date" with Asher because I don't want to build it up in my head and end up disappointed. On Sunday, I get the lowdown on what happened at the winter formal. Bridget did get plastered, and Helena realized it was a mistake to go with Shannon because he spent half the night trying to get her to make out with him. She skipped the after-party and watched *An Affair to Remember* at home, which, according to her, was much more pleasurable than formal.

A few hours later, I'm in my car on my way to meet Asher. It has started to snow, a wet snow that leaves water trails down my windshield. Asher lives in a three-story blue house with two gables and a basketball hoop over the garage. It's 3:15—I'm fashionably late. I ring the doorbell and take a deep breath, thinking about how today is the first day of the rest of my life, how right now could be what I'll look back upon as the moment when everything changed.

The door opens. It's not Asher, but his mother. She's tall and has cropped hair and angular shoulders and a round belly and the same deep, brown eyes as Asher. "Nina, come in, come in," she says. I follow her into the kitchen. It's warm and smells like dough and lemons.

"Sit," she tells me. "Would you like something to eat?"

Before I can answer, Asher comes down the stairs.

"Your friend Nina is here," his mother says. "Have a seat."

"We have to do work, Mama," Asher says.

"I baked some rosemary bread." His mother puts a bottle of olive oil and a plate of bread down on the counter in front of me. "First eat, then study."

Asher grabs a piece of bread and pours olive oil all over it. He's wearing gray sweatpants and a Deer Hook High basketball T-shirt and he must have just gotten out of the shower because his hair is damp. Could he have showered for me? "How are your exams going so far?" he asks.

"Oh, I don't know. I'm just happy that my French exam is over." French is the one subject I've never managed to get an A in. So much for the language of love.

"French is a beautiful language," Asher's mother says. "I speak it."

"I should too by now, but I don't," I tell her.

"Asher's told me about you," his mother says. "He says you're a very smart girl." I look down at the bread in my hands. "He told me you are the best student in the math class. Help my son, will you? He's a smart boy, but not so good at numbers. Me, I've always been good at numbers. I don't know what happened to my son."

"Maybe good math genes skip a generation," Asher suggests.

"Maybe you need to study harder," she responds. "You know, Nina, I didn't want to move to Buffalo, but our cousin wanted us to start a restaurant with him so we go. When I finally start to feel like it is home, Asher's father decides we should come here. I told him I didn't want to come. The schools there are better. But he wanted to buy this restaurant in this little town and now Asher is struggling."

"I'm not struggling," Asher protests.

" 'Mama,' he says to me. 'The people in this town are so ignorant about the rest of the world.' "

"You said that, not me," Asher corrects her.

"I'm not a big fan of Deer Hook, either. But maybe it'll grow on you, like Buffalo did," I offer. His mother leans over the counter and pinches my cheek like an auntie.

"You're a sweet girl," she says. "Please teach my Asher some math."

"She would if you'd let us," Asher says.

She holds up her hands. "I'm going, I'm going. I'll be at the restaurant if you need anything. If you get hungry there's some *tonno e fagioli* in the fridge." She tells him something in Italian and he answers back in Italian and she squeezes his shoulder and then she's gone and it's Asher and me and only a plate of rosemary bread between us.

"Should we go up to my room?" Asher asks.

I feel like there's a lump of bread lodged in my throat and start coughing. Asher pats me on the back until my coughing subsides, which luckily takes only a few seconds. "Are you okay?"

"I'm okay," I say. If by "okay" you mean mortified. "Should we head up?"

"Where do your parents think you are?" he inquires as we climb the stairs.

"At a mandatory math final review. I shouldn't stay too long."

On the wall above Asher's bed are posters of individual basketball players wearing USA jerseys with titles like "Court Warrior," "Mailman," and "Playmaker." On his dresser is a picture of his family standing on a blue-and-white-checkered picnic blanket. Asher's a little boy in it, his wavy hair almost to his shoulders and covering half his face, and next to him is a girl who looks like a taller, female version of him. His father has hair that's much curlier than Asher's and square spectacles and is a few inches shorter than his mother, and they all look so relaxed. "I didn't know you had a sister," I comment.

"Yeah, she got married this past September and lives in Italy. I'm going to go see her this summer," he says. He's sitting on top of his bedspread, leaning back on his elbows.

"I have an older sister too."

"I know," Asher says. "We talked about her, remember?"

Duh. Next topic. "You must look forward to going back to Italy."

"Yeah, I do," he says. "Although the States feels like home now."

I take a seat at his desk. The chair and desk are both painted yellow with flowers stenciled around the legs of the chair and the edges of the desk. It looks like he's had it for a while. I imagine a young Asher hunched over this desk learning how to add and subtract. "It must have been hard to move here from Italy."

"Yeah, it was hard, but playing a sport definitely helped me make friends and get adjusted. I don't mind Deer Hook, though. But I don't know if it'll ever grow on my mother. I give my father less than two years before he gets tired of her complaining and agrees to move back to Pisa."

Asher has a globe on his desk, an antique one that's light brown with a brass base. I contemplate telling him about the game I used to play, but I'm too nervous to express anything that would require forming more than a single sentence.

"Should we get to work?" he asks.

I nod. Getting to work means that we should probably be closer together, so I stand up and Asher shifts over on the bed so I can sit down next to him. There are only about two feet between us. We go

over the problems and for a while Asher is resting his hand on the
bed so close to mine our pinkies almost meet. I don't tell Asher this,
but I already went over the problems last night, and I let him do most
of the calculations.

"You probably think I'm so slow," he says when we're done.

"You're not slow," I tell him, though he's definitely slower than
me.

"You're just being nice." He gently elbows me in the side, our first
physical contact since the time our knees touched on the bus. The
bus. My stripe. Argh. "Pakistan," he says. "What's that like?"

"I don't know, I've never been, but I'm going there soon."

"Well, change is always good, right?"

"That's easier to believe if you know what the change will be like.
But, at the very least, it'll be interesting."

Asher nods, and we're both quiet for a second.

"Those are really nice earrings," he says. I touch one of the earrings, which I wore today for good luck. "I remember you were wearing them when you came to the diner on your birthday."

"You remember that?"

"Yeah. That's kind of crazy, right?" he says. I nod, and then we're
both silent.

"Are you still hungry? My mom left us more food in the fridge."

I shake my head.

"I have to apologize for my mother. She can be a little melodramatic." He puts his hand to his forehead. " 'In Pisa, I had my family
and friends and a terrace overlooking the Arno, and here, here the
only scenery is loneliness!' "

"She says that?"

Asher smiles for a second, flashing his cutie gap at me. "Something like that, except in Italian."

"My mother's really melodramatic too. 'Nina, you can't talk to boys because if you do you'll get pregnant!' "

Asher laughs. "Does she really say that?"

"Something like that, except in Urdu." I'm not sure, but I swear that the distance between me and Asher has become a little less, and he's looking right at me with those melt-in-your-mouth chocolate eyes. I curl my fingernails against the bedspread and try to send subliminal messages. Asher Richelli, you will kiss me. You will kiss me. You will—

Asher's head is tilted and coming toward me and his eyes are half-closed and oh my God he is actually going to kiss me and I can't close my eyes, I can only watch him coming, and, right as our noses are about to touch, I jump up.

"I have to go home," I say. "I'm late. Bye!" As I run down the stairs and out the door I can't tell if he's calling after me or not because all I can hear is my heart, which is pumping like someone injected my aorta with adrenaline, reverberating in my ears. I don't dare look back because I'm sure Asher is watching my mad dash to the car from his window, questioning the sanity of the girl he just tried to kiss.

Find Out What It Means to Me

When I arrive at school, Bridget and Helena are already there. I was too nervous to tell them about Asher over the phone at home and instructed them to get to school early. They're sitting on the hood of Bridget's car, huddled together with one of Helena's shawls that her mother got her from Morocco wrapped around their shoulders and passing a red thermos back and forth. As I approach, Bridget says, "This better be good, because I woke up at 6:45 a.m. and you know how much I need my sleep during this stressful time of year."

"Why are you sitting out here?" I ask.

"Helena has decided she needs to prepare for how cold it'll be in the Alps and because of this we must all suffer with her," Bridget explains.

"What happened?" Helena asks. "Is everything okay?"

I tell them, beginning with the math assignment and ending with my freak-out. When I woke up this morning I tried to convince myself that yesterday's debacle wasn't such a big deal, but now, after relaying the story and seeing the looks on their faces—astonishment and shock (and a tiny bit of amusement on Bridget's part)—I feel like an idiot, through and through.

"Let me get this straight," Bridget says. "Asher Richelli, who you haven't been able to shut up about for months, finally tries to kiss you and you scream bloody murder and run away?"

"I didn't scream. I just ran."

"Oh, Nina. Why?" Helena asks.

"Have you ever wanted something so badly, and then, when it actually happens, you feel like you're going blind and the only way to save your vision is to run like hell?" Blank faces. I forgo the metaphoric for the literal. "I was willing him to kiss me, and then when I realized he was actually going to, I had a flight response."

"I understand. I remember how nervous I was during my first kiss," Helena offers.

"It's cool, Nina," Bridget says. "Everyone freaks out once in a while. You just have to keep it together the next time it happens."

"Except I don't think it's going to happen again," I say.

"Why are you guys sitting outside?" It's Serena, the last person I want to see in my wretched state. "And what are you talking about so intensely?" She's hugging herself and looking at us huddled beneath the shawl and I hope she doesn't ask if she can share it with us because there's not enough to go around.

"Asher tried to kiss Nina and she ran away," Bridget tells her. As soon as she says this she realizes her big mouth has struck again and widens her eyes at me in an apology.

"Really?" Serena says. Now it's her turn to be shocked and astonished. "Is that true?" I nod. Great. Serena claims she's over Asher, but for all I know, she's already plotting how she's going to get even with me. "Do you know how many girls are dying for Asher to kiss them? I mean, I'm not, of course, but at least half the school is." She snaps her gum. "Fancy that. Asher tried to kiss you! Who would have thought?"

"I thought," Helena answers. "Why wouldn't he like Nina? She's lovely."

This is becoming torturous. "Let's talk about something else, please," I beg.

"There's a simple solution to this," Bridget announces. "What you have to do now is go ahead and kiss him."

"I really don't think I can do that," I say.

Serena shrugs. "You shouldn't, then. Asher will get over it. Are you ready to review for psych, Bridget?" Bridget gets up, mouthing "sorry" to me before she goes.

"You think Serena is pissed?" I ask Helena.

"I don't think so. I think this Rory fellow has finally allowed her to get over Asher," she says.

"I really messed up, didn't I?"

"Of course not! Asher must like you, otherwise he wouldn't have tried to kiss you. Stop berating yourself. Next time you see him, flirt with him. A lot."

"But I'm an awful flirt. You've got your coyness and Bridget has her brashness and I've got—what? Awkwardness? Inexperience? Neither of those is very attractive."

"All you have to do is be yourself. Smile at him. And address him by his name a few times. Boys like that."

I get to precalc early and formulate my brilliant plan, which is less of a plan and more of a desperate attempt to normalize relations between us. When I see Asher walk into our exam, I will smile very widely at him and say, "Hi, Asher," as if nothing ever happened. But when he actually enters, I can't bring myself to look up at him. Instead I start to etch my initials into the desk.

"I wouldn't have pegged you as a vandalist," Mr. Porcupine comments. He's going around the room collecting the problem sets and I hadn't realized he was right next to me. I drop my pencil.

"I don't think that's a word," I tell him.

Mr. Porcupine laughs. "Good thing I'm teaching math, then, not English," he says, winking at me.

I'd promised myself that, no matter how nervous I was, I would force myself to talk to Asher after the exam, but it turns out to be a lot easier than I had imagined because as soon as we're dismissed, Asher taps me on the shoulder. "Hey, Nina," he says. "Can we talk?"

I nod. Smile, Nina. Say his name. Smile. We walk down the hall together, and when we reach the end he turns to me. "Listen," he tells me. "I wanted to apologize." He hesitates. There are now three beautiful crinkles in his forehead. If only I could stand on my tiptoes and kiss each one of them. "I should have known better than to do that. I mean, how many times have you explained to me what your parents are like? Yesterday I put you in an uncomfortable position and it was unfair and I was being selfish and not thinking about you and I'm really sorry."

It takes me a second to process what he's saying. He thinks I'm upset with him, that I didn't kiss him because to kiss him would be to defy my parents and that's something that I don't want to do. Now is my chance—I should correct him, admit I like him, that I in fact do want to kiss him, that I freaked out, that I'm the one who's sorry. "It's okay," I reassure him. "Don't worry about it."

"I didn't mean to be disrespectful," he continues. "I want you to know that."

"I totally understand." There are tears forming somewhere behind my eyes. "I have to go to study hall."

"See you later."

But instead of going to study hall I head to the cafeteria, which is empty except for Hal, the janitor, who Bridget calls General Hal because he has a white beard and mustache like Robert E. Lee's. The cafeteria tables have long benches for seats and I sit down and rest my head in my hands. It's better this way, I tell myself. What would kissing Asher have accomplished except make you feel sad that you can't really go out with him? Now, at least, you're on good terms and he doesn't think you're a freak for running away.

"Are you all right?" It's Hal.

I don't lift my head. "Cramps."

"You should be in the nurse's office, not here."

I sit up and look at him. "Why am I so scared to tell him how I feel? Why am I such a coward?"

General Hal takes a step back. "I have to finish mopping," he says, and takes off as if he just found out I'm the carrier of some lethal virus.

I should have taken Asher by the shoulders. I should have said, "No, you're wrong. The truth is I'm dying to kiss you. Disrespect me, please."

I wish I could go back in time and change it. I wish I was anyone but me.

The Wrath of Khan

English final. Ms. Tazinski has decided to squeeze in a quick lecture about the use of color in *The Great Gatsby*, but I can't pay attention because I swear I can feel Serena casting me evil sideways glances from across the room, though I'm too scared to actually look in her direction to confirm whether this is true or not.

The confirmation I was too fearful to seek out comes at the end of the day, in the form of bubble-gum head marching right up to me. I'm at my locker, unarmed except for the biology textbook in my hand.

"Hi, Nina," Serena says. Her nose doesn't move, which for some reason makes me even more apprehensive.

"Hey."

"Rory and I had an amazing time in New York City," she tells me. She reaches into her pink leather purse and pulls out a silver key chain. "He bought me this from Tiffany's. Isn't it adorable?"

"Um, yeah, as far as key chains go." I'm hoping that this is it, that she cornered me simply so she could boast about her stupid key chain. "Well, I should get going."

"Wait," she says. "I wanted to talk to you about something."

I brace myself for what I'm certain will be some sort of confrontation. I shut my locker with a bang. It's about time I stopped allowing her to intimidate me. "What?"

A strand of her hair is stuck to her shiny lip gloss and she brushes it away before beginning. "I was wondering if you think it's really a good idea to pursue Asher when you're not even allowed to date. Like, what do you hope to accomplish? Shouldn't you let a girl who can actually be with him have him?"

"What are you talking about? Do you still like him? I thought you were in love with Rory."

"Oh, I totally am," she says. "I'm thinking of Asher, not me. Even though Asher and I decided to break up, he's the nicest guy and I would hate to see him get hurt."

As I recall, Asher's the one who dumped her, but I don't see any purpose in challenging her revisionist history. Even though Serena is making a point I've thought about myself, the anger is rising in my stomach. I'm trying hard to keep it there and not let it erupt out of my mouth. "Look, there's nothing going on between us anyway, but even if there was, I don't see why it's any of your business. And just because I can't date doesn't mean I'm not allowed to have feelings for another human being."

"I'm not saying that. I don't want to see either of you get hurt, that's all. It's only some friendly concern," she insists, blue eyes wide under a thick layer of mascara that's tinted her eyelashes pitch-black.

"That would make sense if we were friends," I tell her.

She blows a tiny pink bubble from the side of her lips. "Really, Nina, you don't have to be such a bitch."

That's it. No more holding back my anger. Call me Mount Vesuvius. "You're calling me a bitch?" I practically yell this and a few people down the hall turn around to look. "Isn't that the irony of the week!"

"What is that supposed to mean?"

"You're the bitch, Serena. You've been a bitch to me since we were little."

"What are you talking about?"

"Remember the time in third grade when you told everyone my family eats monkey brains like in *Indiana Jones and the Temple of Doom*? And the time at Bridget's birthday party when you told everyone to listen to me pee?"

Serena blinks. "I don't remember that." Not remember? How could she not remember the slings and arrows she aimed directly at the Achilles heel of my soul? "And, I mean, even if I did do that, that was such a long time ago," she continues. "We were kids. Kids say dumb things. I always used to get asked if I lived with the animals at the zoo. Shouldn't you be over it by now?"

As if it were that easy. "Every time you see me you wrinkle your nose."

Serena's cheeks burn red under her pink blush. "That's funny, because every time I try to hang out with Bridget and Helena when you're around you sit there with this pissed-off expression on your face. I'd love to hang out with Bridget and Helena more and I can't because you don't like me."

"Oh, please. You get to see them all the time on weekends."

"If you didn't hate me so much, I'd be better friends with them," she says.

"I don't hate you."

"You're not better than everyone else because you get good grades," she continues.

When did this conversation turn into an outright assassination of my character? "I don't think that. How could I? I'm the one who's the freak around here, remember?"

"You're not a freak," she says. "I mean, you could use a nicer hair-style and better fashion sense, but you're not a freak."

In Serena's world, I suppose this passes for a compliment. Part of me is still infuriated, but part of me wonders if her accusations are true—do I sit there looking pissed off whenever she's present? Does she really envy my friendships so much? Is the grass over there not quite as green as I thought?

"Look, I'm sorry for whatever I might have said when we were little that upset you," she tells me. "I didn't come over here to start a fight."

"Well, I do like Asher," I declare. "And if you have a problem with that, it's too bad."

"I don't have a problem with it," Serena says. "I'm done with high school boys."

"Good. I'm glad you met someone you like," I say, and I mean it, even if mostly for the sake of my personal health and safety.

"Good luck with Asher." She doesn't sound 100 percent sincere when she says it, but I suppose the fact that she even said it is a step in the "perhaps we are not mortal enemies after all" direction.

I nod and watch her walk away, and for the first time, I catch a glimpse of Serena, the girl who may actually have a heart hidden deep within her. Now that I know that I've got a patch of grass that looks pretty good to her, it couldn't hurt to be a little nicer to her when she's around. Serena and I are never going to be friends, but maybe, if she ceases her nose-wrinkles and I cease my pissy expressions, we could achieve an unprecedented level of civility. And my friends call me a pessimist.

Ammi and Abbu

My parents are leaving tomorrow for Pakistan, and our guest room has been the trip packing headquarters for the last few weeks. There's eight suitcases total, two for each of us. Some of them are half empty, waiting to be filled with all of the clothes and jewelry and decorative items my mother plans to bring to Pakistan, and some of them are full, with *shalwar kameez* and shoes and a Ziploc full of medicines and packaged dress shirts and colognes and perfumes and ties and bags of candy to give as gifts to our various relatives and their children because apparently you have to bring a gift for everyone. I'm helping my mother with the last-minute packing, and just the sight of all the suitcases and their contents is a little overwhelming. I have a feeling that there'll be nothing minimalist about Pakistan, that this is only the beginning. But I'm looking forward to being in someplace so completely different, even if everyone does laugh at my Urdu.

One of the suitcases isn't closing so I sit on top of it as my mother tries to zip it again.

"What's happened to this room?"

Sonia is standing in the doorway. "Sonia!" my mother cries. "You're back!" She opens up her arms and Sonia carefully makes her way through the luggage and steps into the embrace. She's got shadows the color of charcoal underneath her eyes.

"I'm exhausted," she announces. "I had to finish my assignments early so I could come home to babysit."

"I'm not a baby," I retort.

"No fighting," my mother tells us. "All right. I'm almost done packing. You two are bringing the four blue suitcases. There's lots of food in the fridge, enough for a week. And make sure you don't tell anyone you're home without your parents."

Sonia laughs. "Why, in case the Deer Hook cat burglar decides to strike?"

"What cat burglar?" my mother says.

"I'm kidding. We'll be fine, Ma. I'll take good care of Nina."

I stick my tongue out at her when my mother's not looking. "I can take good care of myself, thank you very much."

"Well, excuse me, then," Sonia says.

"I said no fighting," my mother admonishes us. "You have to take care of each other. My girls." She hugs both of us so tightly I can feel the cartilage of Sonia's ear pressed against my neck. "Why don't you two get dinner ready?"

"Okay, but after dinner I'm going straight to bed," Sonia says. "I'm beat."

I follow Sonia into the kitchen. She opens up the fridge and takes out the Tupperware containers. "You set the table and I'll warm these up," she commands.

"Why don't you set the table and I'll warm these up?" I reply. I wouldn't mind setting the table, but she can't walk in here and order me around like I'm still a little kid. If the main determinant of whether or not you belong to a place is the amount of time you spend there, then this is more my house than hers.

"What's your problem?" Sonia asks.

"I don't have a problem."

One of Sonia's tiny hands is now perched on her tiny hip, and I prepare for an argument, but she says, "That's okay. I'm sure your exams must be stressing you out. How are they going?"

"Fine. I'm going to be up all night studying."

Sonia nods. "How's everything else?"

"Fine."

We work in silence for the rest of the time. My father walks in. "I miss you two already!" he says. He pulls a hundred-dollar bill out of his pocket and gives it to Sonia.

"But Ma already left some money for us," Sonia tells him.

He puts his finger to his lips. "Take your sister out for dinner and a movie."

Great. The only person I get to go on a date with is my sister, and that's only because someone else is paying for it.

"Or you can go shopping, buy some books," my father adds. "You'll need books to read on the plane. And you should bring some snacks with you because the plane food is pretty bad. Although maybe things have changed. I haven't been to Pakistan in such a long time. I wonder what it will feel like to be there again." He pauses, and his eyes are looking past us, at something far away.

"I'm sure it will feel different," Sonia says. "But in a good way. Right, Nina?"

"Right," I concur, and my father smiles and gives both Sonia and me a hug. Apparently it's Group Embrace Day in the Khan family.

All through dinner my mother makes lists and gives us instructions: to confirm our pickup with the airport car service; to make sure to lower the heat before we leave because there's no point in wasting money; that after we get our luggage at Karachi Airport we will be accosted by many coolies trying to take our bags but to make sure that we hold on to them; that she and Dad and Nasreen Khala and Khalu will come to the airport to greet us so before we land we should brush our teeth and our hair and look presentable; that we must make sure to say *salaam* to everyone; that when we go shopping let her do the talking because the shopkeepers will know that we aren't from there and charge us higher prices; that in Pakistan we should call them *Ammi* and *Abbu*, not Ma and Dad, because that's the correct way to address your parents; that we should make a point of talking to everyone otherwise people might think we are stuck-up Americans.

Good Lord. We haven't even gotten to Pakistan yet and already I feel jet-lagged.

"Stuck-up Americans?" Sonia repeats. "Are you serious?"

"Just be friendly," my mother says. "And let everyone know how nice you think Pakistan is."

"But what if I don't think it's nice?" I ask.

"Why wouldn't you?" she responds. "It's crowded and polluted and you'll probably eat something that makes you sick, but it will be very nice to be there."

The next afternoon, after several more hugs and a hundred more instructions, a black Lincoln Town Car is waiting outside and my father and the driver are loading it up with suitcases and my mother is bidding us goodbye. The whole scene seems very dramatic, as if we're not going to see them for months instead of one week. "We'll call you as soon as we arrive," my mother says. "Take care of each other."

Sonia and I promise we will, and then they're gone. We go up to our rooms. I shut my door, and Sonia shuts hers, and the only indication that there's someone else in the house besides me is the new toothbrush in the bathroom.

Embrace Each Day with Spirit Deep

When I get home from school on Wednesday, Sonia is curled up on the leather recliner in the family room, reading a book. "How did the exams go?" she asks.

"All right." I flop down on the sofa. "What are you reading? The Oxford English Dictionary?"

"No," she says, as if it's common for her to read the OED. "It's a travel guide about Pakistan. Did you know Moenjodaro was once the leading metropolis of the Indian subcontinent? I'm so excited to go see it with Khalu."

I put down my backpack and fall onto the sofa. "I feel like I barely know Khalu."

"He's really cool. I still remember this poem he made up for me when I was young. 'Oh little girl, do not sleep / the world will its secrets keep / from those who do not rise and shine / embrace each day with spirit deep.' "

"Khalu wrote you a poem?"

"And he used to eat rose petals. Remember that? He told me if you ate enough of them, they'd make you invisible, and I went out to the backyard and ate like ten petals off of Ma's rosebush and Ma yelled at him. And last time he was here he told me about some army boarding school he went to when he was little and how they had to get up at five every morning and do fifty push-ups in the courtyard."

"He told you all this?" I ask. "I don't remember him telling me anything."

"That's because I actually talked to him," Sonia says. "If you'd stop avoiding your relatives and the aunties and uncles and start conversing with them, you might learn something."

Before I can come up with some kind of retort, the phone rings. It's Bridget. "Guess who's going out tomorrow night?" she says.

"Who?"

"We are!"

"What are you talking about?"

"Shannon Kelly is having a party to celebrate the last day of school."

"But the last day of school is Friday."

"Only freshmen have exams Friday."

"But I wasn't invited."

"It's not a formal-invitation thing, stupid," Bridget says. "This is Shannon we're talking about, remember? And Asher should be there, and, trust me, after you have a drink, you'll stop being such a wuss and finally go up to him and engage in some tongue jousting."

"I'm not promising to do any jousting, but I'll come. Although I guess I should ask my sister."

"She wouldn't say no, would she?"

"I don't think so. She better not."

Bridget whistles. "Get ready, Deer Hook, Nina's stepping out!" She yells this so loudly that I have to hold the receiver away from my ear.

"What was your friend so happy about?" my sister asks after I hang up.

"That was Bridget. She wants me to go with her to a party tomorrow night. Everyone in school is going."

"A party?" Sonia gets off the recliner and walks over to me, her hands clasped behind her back like I'm on the witness stand and she's questioning me. "You know Ma and Dad would never allow you to go to this party."

"What's your point?"

"My point," she says, "is that I have reservations. I'm supposed to take care of you and what if something happens to you at this party?"

"Since when do I need your permission to do something?"

"Why do you even want to go to this party anyway?" she asks. "Weren't you telling me over Thanksgiving how much you hated high school?"

"I never said I hated it. And I'm not saying it's going to be a great party, but for once I'd like to see what these parties that everyone talks about are actually like."

"Are you planning on drinking?"

"Maybe."

Sonia returns to her chair, takes off her glasses, and begins again, her voice softer this time, like I'm now in therapy instead of on trial. "But Nina, don't you think sixteen is too young to drink?"

"Oh, but seventeen is old enough to go live on your own on a college campus where everyone drinks all the time?"

Sonia frowns. "That's different."

"Why? Because at seventeen you were so much more mature than me?"

"That's not what I meant. And you'll be seventeen when you first start college too, you know," she says. She studies her book like she's divining something from the cover photo. "Okay. You're practically an adult and you're a smart person and I'm not going to tell you what to do. But I'm coming to pick you up at one, and I expect you to be in a lucid state. Deal?"

"Lucid is my middle name." I reach out my hand and we shake on it. Sonia may be small, but she's got a really strong grip. Even her handshake is more impressive than mine.

The Archer and the Princess

I try on several different potential party outfits before deciding on my darkest, hence the most slimming, pair of jeans, a black V-neck

T-shirt, and, to dress it up a bit, the black and gold choker Nasreen Khala gave me on her last visit.

Bridget and Anthony pick me up. "Ready for the big night?" Bridget asks me when I get in the car.

"Can you not put any pressure on me? I'm nervous enough as it is."

"Yeah, back off," Anthony says. "These things have to happen naturally."

Bridget snorts. "Naturally, my ass. If I hadn't asked you out, would we even be together right now? Sometimes things only happen if you take the bull by the horns and swing it around your head. You can do it, Nina. Just have a beer and walk up to Asher and just do it."

"She said no pressure, Bridget," Anthony reminds her. Bridget shuts up and I silently thank him for sticking up for me. As much courage as it took Bridget to ask Anthony out, it will take me at least twice as much to kiss Asher. But I figure that if I ever do manage to kiss him, a party is the ideal setting because if it backfires I can always blame my actions on the alcohol. "You look really nice, Nina. Doesn't she, Bridget?" Anthony says.

"Smokin'," Bridget says. "Speaking of smoking, my mother is finally trying to quit and she's such a pain to be around now."

Bridget keeps complaining about her mother, but I'm too nervous and can't pay attention. I'm trying to visualize kissing Asher but I only get as far as leaning toward him before I start freaking out.

By the time we get to Shannon's house it's already packed. I nod at the people I recognize from school. A few of them do double-takes when they see me, but I choose to ignore this.

"Where are Shannon's parents, anyway?" I ask.

"How do I know? Am I his keeper?" Bridget says. "Come on. Shannon's mother told him no booze in the house so he said he's going to put the keg in the backyard. Cheeky, right?"

I follow her through the kitchen, where two sophomores are having a chugging contest while people form a circle around them and chant, "Go, Go, Go." So much for no booze in the house.

"Nina!" Shannon Kelly steps in front of me, sloshing beer in hand. "What are you doing here?"

"Nina wouldn't miss your big party," Bridget says.

"Yeah!" Shannon cries, waving his free hand in the air. "Nina likes to party!"

"He's wasted," Bridget whispers in my ear. That much is obvious. I may not have hung out with many drunk people, but that doesn't mean I don't know one when I see one.

"Hey, man," Shannon greets Anthony. "What's up?"

"What's up?" Anthony nods.

Shannon puts his hand on Anthony's shoulder. "I got to tell you, man, one of my favorite baseball players of all time is Willie Mays. That dude was awesome."

"That's fascinating, Shannon, but we need to get some drinks," Bridget says, and we continue our journey through the kitchen. The two sophomores are now on their second chugging contest. No sign of Asher yet.

The keg is indeed in the backyard and there's a circle of people surrounding it. The social geometry of this party is definitely biased toward circles. Helena's sitting on a wooden bench and I head over to her after Anthony promises to procure a drink for me. "You look great!" she says.

"Thanks. So is this what all these parties are like?"

"Pretty much," she says. "Did you see how wasted Shannon is? It's so unattractive. You'd think that after I consistently refused to kiss him at winter formal, he would get the hint. But he tried to kiss me again tonight and I pushed him away and he was so drunk he fell on the ground and started laughing. I should never have said yes to him in the first place. I only did it because everyone kept asking me who I was going to formal with and I figured I ought to go. As God is my witness, I'm not going on another date until I meet a boy who is mature and confident and intelligent and sensitive and strong."

"Well, Scarlett, good luck meeting one of those at Deer Hook High," I say.

"I know. Then again, you met Asher." She nudges me. "Have you seen him yet?"

"No sign."

"One beer for the lady," Anthony says, walking up to us. As he's about to give it to me Bridget comes up from behind and takes it from his hand.

"Listen, Nina," she begins. "You better not drink more than one beer, otherwise you might end up puking on Asher instead of making out with him."

"Maybe Nina shouldn't have any beer," Helena says. "I mean, don't you think it's better to be sober for your first kiss? That way you're in touch with all five of your senses, and you can really revel in it."

"If Nina doesn't have a little bit to drink there isn't going to be a first kiss," Bridget responds. "She can 'revel' in their second kiss, right, Nina?"

I can tell Helena is about to refute this, so I cut her off. "Stop arguing and give me the beer," I demand, and Bridget hands it to me.

"What would your parents say if they saw you now?" Helena asks.

"Oh, they'd never understand; they've never had a drink in their life. But I don't think it's morally wrong like they do." I take a sip. "This tastes awful."

"Cheap beer usually does," Helena says.

"It's better if you drink it fast," Bridget tells me.

I wipe the foam off my lips. "I don't know if I can drink it at all. It tastes like cow piss."

"Just drink a little, then," Bridget suggests.

"Did you hear Shannon's comment about Willie Mays? Like I'm supposed to congratulate him or something?" Anthony says. "That kid is such an idiot."

Helena shakes her head. "Tell me about it."

Bridget pushes her cup against mine. "To first kisses!" I go for the faster-is-better approach and take a huge gulp, grimacing at the taste. Then I take another.

"Easy there, tiger," Anthony says.

"It tastes so bad I want to finish it quickly," I explain. "Has anyone seen Asher?"

"Should we go look for him?" Helena suggests.

I nod and stand up, but I feel a little unsteady and sit back down. "My bearings," I say. I wait a couple of seconds before attempting vertical again, and this time my bearings cooperate.

"Let's go dance," Bridget says. We go inside and Bridget and Anthony head to the living room where some people are dancing in a circle and others are sprawled out on the couches. Helena and I stand in the hallway between the kitchen and the living room.

"How do you feel?" she asks.

"I think I'm already a little drunk," I say, finishing my beer.

"Be careful," she warns me. "And let me know if you see Shannon coming. I keep worrying he might try a sneak attack."

"Let me know if you see Asher," I say.

Helena leaves me to go to the bathroom and I wander back into the kitchen to get some water.

"Nina?" It's Robbie Nash, Mr. Volunteer Society himself. He's towering over almost everyone in the room. I'd never realized how long he really is—Abraham Lincoln long: long body, long nose, long fingers.

"Happy birthday, Mr. President," I say, trying to make my voice as hoarse as possible. I think I'm being really witty, but Robbie's lips remain in one long, straight, unamused line.

"What are you doing here?" he asks.

I raise my empty cup. "Same thing as you." I feel like I'm talking really loud, but the room we're in is really loud; in fact, it's so loud in here that I'm probably not talking loud enough.

"Are you drunk? I didn't even know you drank." He seems concerned.

"I don't. But I did. Tonight, that is. *Je buvais, j'ai bu, j'avais bu.* I am so glad I get a break from French, aren't you?"

"I'm taking Spanish."

"I don't know much Spanish," I say. *"Buenos noches?"*

"Buenas noches," he corrects me. I want to ask him if he's always so serious but he probably wouldn't find this funny. I wonder what he's thinking about. Something long, probably, like a redwood tree. "Well, nice seeing you," he says, and takes off.

"Nina! What's up!" Shannon screams in my ear. He's holding two beers and hands me one. "This is especially for you, baby. Bottoms up!" The cup he gave me doesn't have that much beer inside and I drink it in one go. When I finish I see that Shannon hasn't touched his.

"Made you drink!" he cries.

"Shannon, I have something I want to say to you," I tell him. "I'm not Indian."

"You're funny," he says. "Not funny in a bad way."

"Funny in a good way," I say, and Shannon nods vigorously, thrilled that I understand. It's hopeless. Then Shannon pours some of his beer into my cup, spilling a little on my hand, and takes off.

"Hey, you just missed your lover boy," I inform Helena when she returns from the bathroom.

"Thank God. Did I miss anything else?"

"I think I scared away Robbie Nash."

Helena laughs.

"I love you, you know that?" I tell her.

"You are getting drunk!" she says. "But I love you too. And speaking of love, have you seen Asher?"

I shake my head. Anthony walks over and tells us we should come dance, so we follow him into the living room. I finish my beer en route and then I have to hold on to the wall as I walk because it's helping me keep my balance. The song "Jump Around" is playing and everyone's screaming "Jump! Jump! Jump!" and jumping up and down so hard the wooden floor is shaking. It's making me feel sick and I need to go outside for some fresh air. I try to tell my friends, but they're already lost in the crowd so I turn around and forge my way through the kitchen, where I keep my head down because I figure if I don't make eye contact with anyone they can't really see me. I finally make it out to the backyard and pause on the back steps, inhaling. Cold air never felt so good.

I continue down the steps, holding on to the railing. At the bottom of the stairs I am very sad to let the railing go, but I have no choice. I walk across the backyard, trying not to stumble, avoiding the area around the keg where the people are, and head toward the weeping willow tree. The moon is only half full and I think about how great it would be if the moon was full and surrounded by stars and if Asher and I could make out up in the sky like two constellations in love. He would be an archer, and I would be a princess at a loom. There's something very sexy about a woman at a loom. Except I don't know how to weave so I would have to fake it, or learn somehow. I wish I was a country on Asher's antique globe and then he could spin it and his finger could land on me. "Not Brazil, me," I say aloud. The sky looks like it's changing colors, and the ground looks like it's grown to the height of my knees, and then I realize that this is because I'm on my knees, and suddenly everything goes black.

Little and Big

When I open my eyes I'm on a bed in a room covered in New York Mets posters. "She's awake!" Helena says. She, Bridget, and Anthony are standing over me.

I sit up. "How long have I been out?"

"Not long," Bridget says.

"How did I get here?"

"I carried you," Anthony says.

"Asher?" I ask.

Helena shakes her head. "He never showed up. Probably had to work late at the restaurant."

"Thank God for that."

"Drink this." Helena hands me a mug that says "Thank You, Lord, for Making Me Irish."

"You had more than one beer, didn't you?" Bridget asks. I nod. "I told you not to have more than one, Miss Lightweight."

"Lay off, Bridget. She's had a rough enough night as it is," Anthony says.

I look around but can't see a clock. "What time is it?"

"Almost one," Bridget says.

"Great." I groan. "Sonia's going to give me the biggest lecture."

"Good," Bridget says. "Maybe next time it'll make you think twice before you chug away."

"As I recall," Helena says, "you were the one who told her that she should have a beer in the first place."

"I wanted her to have one beer so she could loosen up a little, not black out!" Bridget snaps.

"Can you guys not add to my suffering by fighting, please?" I drink all of the water. "I should go outside to wait for Sonia."

"We'll go with you," Helena says. She holds my arm as I walk and Bridget and Anthony follow behind. I feel like I've just been discharged from a hospital. In the living room, the music has stopped and been replaced by snores and giggles. There are a bunch of people on the couches, some passed out, a few of them lip-locked. One of the couples making out is Shannon Kelly and Cassie Banks. "She's alive!" Shannon yells when he sees me, but thankfully that's the extent of it because Cassie pulls his head back toward hers.

The air feels good inside my nose and throat and I close my eyes for a second, trying to sober up as much as I can. I hear a car drive up and don't have to open my eyes to know it's Sonia.

Sonia steps out of the car. "Hello, everyone." Something about the way she's wrapped up in her brown wool coat makes her look like a very serious mouse.

"Hi," Helena and Bridget say in unison.

"Was the party fun?" Sonia asks, eyeing me.

"Yes." I figure it's better to come clean. "I drank a little too much, I think."

"Really." She nods once, then gets back into the car.

Bridget and Helena give me a hug and say they'll call me tomorrow and Anthony helps situate me in the car and even buckles my seat belt and Sonia looks supremely annoyed. Party over. Game over. Goal not obtained.

"I thought we had a deal," Sonia says. She looks funny when she drives. Her shoulders are hunched and she's sitting so close to the wheel it looks like it's growing out of her chest.

I feel wavy and my head hurts. "I'm lucid. I swear."

"How many beers did you have, anyway?"

"Like two. Maybe three."

She shakes her head slowly. "Do you know what an amazing thing the human consciousness is? Why would you even want to impair it?"

"Please don't yell at me."

"I'm not yelling. I'm just telling you that if you decide to do something like this again, you should really make sure that you're doing it for the right reasons, not just because you want to rebel or fit in."

After spending most of her visits home ignoring me, I don't see what gives her the license to lecture me like this. "You know, Sonia, I find it really interesting that you suddenly think you can tell me how I should behave. For the past few years you've been so absorbed in your, like, oh so wonderful new life that you pretty much forgot you even had a sister! It must have been a surprise every time you came home to visit and remembered I existed!"

Sonia pulls over to the side of the road. "Is that really what you think? That I forgot about my own sister?"

"No. I don't know." I massage my temples and Sonia waits. "It's not like you've ever bothered to find out how my life was after the puberty monster gobbled me up and spat me out in chunks."

"Well, whenever I call home, I don't recall you ever asking Ma for the phone. You never seemed to want to talk to me. So why do I bear the responsibility for the state of our relationship?"

"Because you're older," I say.

Sonia takes a deep breath, relaxing her shoulders. "Fine. Let's look ahead instead of backward and agree to work on this together. And we should agree to be patient. Relationships don't change overnight."

I'm embarrassed and thirsty and hungry and I've never been good at emotional heart-to-hearts. "That sounds like a plan," I say. "Why did you pull over?"

"I don't like to drive when I'm upset." She starts the car. I close my eyes but that makes me feel worse so I look at my feet instead, my big, size-ten monster feet.

"Sonia? Can I ask you something?"

"As long as it's not antagonistic."

"How come you're so little and I'm so big?"

Sonia laughs. "You are not big, and I'm not that little."

"Yes, you are."

"I've always wished I was taller. You should consider yourself lucky."

"I'm not lucky. I'm stuck in the cytoplasm and Asher will never try to kiss me again."

"Who's Asher?"

"A boy that I like."

"You like a boy named Asher? There's one step toward Middle East peace."

"What do you mean?"

"Asher was a leader of one of the twelve tribes of Israel. He was one of the sons of the Prophet Jacob—we call him Prophet Yaqub."

"How come you know everything?"

Sonia smiles. "Trust me, there's a lot I don't know." We drive into our garage. "We made it!" she says. She seems even more relieved than I am to be home.

"Finally." The pain is still reverberating in my head and on top of it all I'm now hungry, but I don't have it in me to fix something to eat so I head straight to my room. When I get into bed I don't think I've ever been happier to be there in my whole life and I give my mattress a hug. "I love you," I tell it, and somehow I know that it loves me too.

Matchmaker, Matchmaker,
Make Me a Match

I'm woken up by someone shaking my shoulder. "Go away, Ma," I
say.

"It's Sonia."

I open my eyes. Sonia is sitting on my bed, a blue ceramic bowl in
her hands. "I brought you some bananas and honey. My old room-
mate Patty used to claim it was the best hangover cure ever."

"What time is it?" I ask.

"Eleven," Sonia says, handing me a glass of water. "How do you
feel?"

I close my eyes, assess my physical state. Aside from the dehydra-
tion and slight throbbing in the front of my head, I feel fine. "I'm
starving," I say, and start eating the bananas.

"Ma called."

"What did she say?"

"She said they're having a great time. Every night they're invited
to some relative's house for dinner, and apparently we've been invited
to three different weddings while we're there."

By now I've inhaled half of the bananas, and Patty may be onto
something, because I definitely feel rejuvenated. "Wow. That sounds
intense."

"No kidding. Apparently Ma visited the street she grew up on and
she can't even recognize it anymore, it's changed so much," Sonia
says. "She wanted to talk to you but I told her we'd call her later."

"Thanks for having my back."

"That's what sisters are for, right?" Sonia says, and I remember our conversation in the car. "So tell me more about this Asher guy."

"There's nothing to tell." I mean, I am really happy she's making an effort, but I'd rather the whole getting-to-know-you process not start with me revealing the intimate details of my life.

"There must be something," Sonia insists.

"He's this guy at school, and I liked him all semester, but he had a girlfriend for some of it. When he finally tried to kiss me I freaked out and ran away, and we haven't really hung out since."

"He wouldn't have tried to kiss you if he wasn't interested in you, right? But, Nina, maybe it's better this way. I mean, you could try to have some clandestine relationship with this guy, but don't you think it would just be a distraction from more important things, like your college applications?"

"Oh, it's all so moot I don't even need advice," I tell her. Especially from her—the most time she's probably spent with a guy is when she isolated the Y chromosome in some petri dish.

She tucks her knees into her chest and I marvel yet again at how compact my sister can become. "You think I don't have any advice to give about guys because I don't date."

"I didn't say that."

"Dating may not be one of my priorities, but that doesn't mean I don't know anything about boys. I have lots of friends who are guys."

I picture Sonia and a bunch of nerdy guys sitting around a table discussing the latest advances in nuclear physics. "Sonia? Can I ask you a question? What do you do for fun?"

"For fun?" she repeats. "I do lots of things. My friends and I go to this trivia night every Thursday. I go to the movies. I've got season tickets to the repertory theater. When it's warm out I like to Rollerblade along the Charles River."

"You Rollerblade?"

She frowns at me, her eyebrows pulling together. "Why do you seem so surprised? You didn't think I had any fun, did you? Just because I don't drink or date doesn't mean I don't have fun!"

"I know that," I say. "It's not that I don't think you have any fun, but you seem so, so *good*."

"And *good* people don't have fun?"

Everything I'm saying is only deepening the hole I've dug for myself. Sonia seems genuinely hurt by my impression of her life. "I'm sorry," I tell her. "It didn't come out the way I meant it. I know you have a very fulfilling life. I envy it, in fact."

"Why? For all your complaining, you're enjoying high school a lot more than I ever did."

"That's because you never took your nose out of a book in high school," I say.

Sonia nods. "I'll give you that. But anyway, you haven't answered my question. What are you going to do about Asher?"

"I don't know." I put the pillow over my face. "My life would be so much easier if I were good like you."

"Liking a boy doesn't make you bad, silly," she says. "It makes you human. And just because something isn't right for me doesn't make it not right for you. You have to make your own informed choices."

Before she starts giving me a lecture about how one makes truly informed choices, I switch to a topic that I know will divert her attention. "Ma asked me if I would encourage you to start thinking about marriage."

"What? So this is her new tactic, trying to make you her little minion!" Sonia's cheeks start to puff. "It's not going to get better, it's only going to get worse and worse."

"What do you mean?"

"Every time I talk to Ma these days she insists on bringing up marriage. I tell her I'm too young, and she says I don't have to get married now. I can simply get engaged and get married after medical school. And she gives me examples of how so-and-so auntie's daughter got engaged and she's a senior in college, or what a nice girl Huma is and how happy she made her mother by getting married, and then she goes on and on about how the good boys will be taken. 'You better make sure to get one while supplies last!' " Sonia puts her hand on her hip, black eyes glistening. "She's always telling me about some boy she wants to give my number to. It's like we're commodities, like marriage is some free-market transaction and Ma is some kind of broker."

"Have you ever met any of these boys?" I ask.

"I have," she says. "Remember that guy Ma mentioned over Thanksgiving dinner? I agreed, reluctantly, to have dinner with him. He was nice, I guess, but not my type."

"You went on a date with him?"

"Didn't I just say I did?" Sonia snaps.

"And Ma knew?"

"Of course she knew. I went on it because of her!"

"But what about Ma's whole thing about if there's a boy and a girl alone together, there's a third—"

"Yes, but apparently Shaitaan makes himself absent if you've reached the age of betrothal and the boy you're alone with could become your Pakistani husband," Sonia explains. "Anyway, we didn't hit it off. He talked about himself the whole time: what residency he wanted to do, what fellowship he wanted to get. The only question he asked me all night was 'I prefer my food to be spicier than this, don't you?' And of course the next day Ma called to ask if I liked him. When I said no, she became upset. 'Why are your standards so high? Why don't you give these boys a chance? Who do you think you are?' " Sonia groans and lies back on my bed. "I mean, how can any kind of relationship grow *organically* with that kind of pressure on it? And then she tells me that when we come back from Pakistan she wants me to meet this matchmaker! A matchmaker! Can you imagine? It's like I went to bed one night as myself and woke up a character in *Fiddler on the Roof*!" She's in such a frenzied state that I half expect her to stand up and start belting out a song. *Arranged Marriage: the Musical*, starring Sonia Khan. I start to laugh, and Sonia looks at me.

"Sorry," I say.

"No need to be sorry, little sister," she says. "You'll be going through this one day too. Enjoy your freshman and sophomore years, because once you become a junior, Ma will start bringing up the *S* word, as in *shaadi*, as in marriage, as in what will become the main topic of conversation between you and her for the rest of your life until you finally do tie the knot."

"Maybe one of these guys she wants you to meet will be cool," I say.

"Look, it's not that I have anything against marrying a Pakistani boy—it'd be great if I could be happy and Ma and Dad could be happy. But it's not that easy to find someone you like in the first place, and then to find someone within a small, specific subgroup is so much harder. And, on top of it all, I don't have time to be meeting these boys. Of all my college years, this one has the most bearing on my academic and professional future."

"You know you'll be considered an old maid at twenty-six."

Sonia picks up a pillow and tosses it at me. "Listen, when it comes to Ma and marriage, I need you to be on my side, okay?"

First my mother asks me to nudge Sonia toward betrothal, now Sonia wants me to join her in *la résistance*. "I don't know how much good it will do, but I'll defend your right to be single," I say.

"Thanks," she says. "Anyway, don't worry about this Asher guy. One day, Ma will have a whole Rolodex of boys waiting to meet you."

We both laugh, nostrils flaring in unison, and the phone rings. Sonia answers. "Hey," she says, and hands it to me. "It's Bridget. I'll be downstairs if you need anything."

"How are you feeling, rock star?" Bridget asks.

"Much better, thanks."

"Have you planned attempt number two with Asher yet?"

"Forget it," I say. "I can't keep chasing Asher—it's like a really bad joke someone tells, and they keep extending and extending it even though it isn't funny. I'm not going to extend the Asher thing anymore. I screwed up, it's over, he's moved on. End of joke."

"Well, the joke's on you, babe."

"What are you talking about?"

"You know how my parents rented that ski house last year? Well, they rented it again this year and guess who's coming up tomorrow and spending the night?"

"Anthony."

"And Helena. And you." Bridget pauses. "And Asher."

"What? Who invited Asher?"

"It was my idea to have you guys up, and Helena called Asher to see if he could come and he said yes. What do you think of that punch line?"

"But I'm leaving for Pakistan on Monday," I say.

"What difference does it make? You'll be back on Sunday, and you're basically all packed, right?"

I'm so nervous and excited, I can't speak.

"Are you still there?"

"But I'm such a terrible skier."

"Who cares? Anthony's never been on skis in his life. Nina, this is your chance. Are you going to seize the bull by the horns or not?"

"That's a leading question. And I should probably check with my sister first."

"Sonia won't mind—tell her my parents will be there the whole time. I'll pick you up tomorrow morning. Oh, and make sure to bring your bathing suit because the house has an awesome hot tub."

My euphoria lasts a few seconds, then instantly tanks when I realize the implications of Bridget's last sentence. Hot tub. Bathing suit. Baring of skin. Bridget and Helena will be wearing bikinis and I'm going to look conspicuously overdressed if I wear a T-shirt and shorts. Somewhere out there, there must be a one-piece bathing suit with enough coverage that I can wear it without subjecting myself to public humiliation. I haul myself out of bed, get in the car, and go bathing suit shopping.

It is, hands down, one of the most painful, depressing, and masochistic activities I have ever voluntarily participated in. "You have a fuller bottom," the saleswoman at one of the stores tells me, which must be the politically correct way of saying that I'm fat from the waist down. "You should try on some skirt bottoms."

But it's not the bottoms I'm having a problem with, it's the tops—neither of the two stores I visit has a bathing suit with a full back that hides my stripe. "You're looking for an athletic suit," another saleswoman explains. "We don't carry those." I finally find a black one-piece I like. It scoops to the middle of my back but I buy it anyway, in the hope that somehow, between now and this weekend, I'll wake up and my stripe will have miraculously disappeared.

Magic Box

When I see Sonia at home I want to complain to her about my stripe, but I'm not quite ready to discuss it with anyone, even my sister. Instead I complain about how fat I look in a bathing suit, and Sonia says, "There's only one solution to this problem. Let's go out for ice cream."

"Have you not been listening to what I'm saying? I can't eat ice cream!"

"Have some frozen yogurt, then. Come on, I've been craving ice cream all day."

We go to Dairy Queen and I end up ordering a chocolate ice

cream cone dipped in chocolate because how can you possibly enter a Dairy Queen and not do such a thing? Sonia and I have a seat in one of the booths to enjoy our indulgences.

"What do you think will happen between you and Asher?" she asks, eating a big spoonful of chocolate ice cream mixed with Snickers and hot fudge. It's really unfair that she can eat anything she wants and stay so small. I don't see why both of us couldn't have inherited my dad's pig-out-with-no-consequences genes.

I lower my voice even though there's no one around to hear us. "I'm trying to avoid having expectations. It'll be nice just to hang out with him." Sonia nods and we eat our ice cream in silence and then I decide to ask her something that's been on my mind. "Hey, Sonia?"

"What?"

"Let's say Asher and I have a great weekend together and let's say we both like each other and we do try to have some clandestine relationship, and let's say Ma and Dad find out. I mean, they'd freak out but they'd still love me, right?"

"What do you think?"

"I think they would, right? But if I did do those things, does that mean I can't be a good Muslim?" I say.

Sonia sticks her spoon back into her ice cream and begins. "Well, what is a good Muslim? Whose definition are you applying to that? In every religion people pick and choose what they want to follow. Look at Ma and Dad's own friends—a few of the aunties cover their hair, and a few of the aunties drink, some fast during Ramadan, some don't. You can't spend your life worrying about what other people will think. If you live decently and help others, is Allah going to condemn you simply because you had a beer? I don't think so, but

SHEBA KARIM

others might. In the end, you have to do what *you* believe is right."

"But what about Ma and Dad?" I say.

"Ma and Dad?" Sonia slides her finger along the edge of the table. "Well, they'd be upset, and disappointed, and probably feel betrayed. And concerned."

I groan and cover my ears. It already sounds like it's not worth it. Sonia takes my wrists and gently pulls my hands down. "But of course they'd still love you, silly," she says.

"Ma told me once that Aziz Uncle's daughter married a white boy and he didn't talk to her for six whole years," I say.

"Nina, you're talking to me as if I have the key to some magical box and I can open it up for you and there, inside, will be the answers to your questions and you'll never have to ponder these matters again. It doesn't work like that. When it comes to these things, religion and orthodoxy and culture and self-actualization, there is no magic box, and there are no easy answers."

I suppose that I knew, long before I asked Sonia these questions, that there wouldn't be any easy answers. But now it's official and on top of that my ice cream cone is almost finished. "Why is life so complicated?"

"Well, brace thyself, because things only get more complicated as you get older. You very well may be wrestling with these questions of faith and morality and guilt for the rest of your life. But who knows, maybe that's a good thing. Sometimes it's our demons that save us, in the end." Sonia reaches over and wipes some chocolate off my chin with a napkin.

"Sonia?"

"Yes, Nina?"

"What do you think I should do? About Asher?"

She shakes her head. "I can't tell you what to do. The only thing I can offer you is a platitude—in matters of love, you should always pay attention to your head, but, ultimately, you must listen to your heart. Maybe that's not the most practical advice, but there it is."

We finish our ice cream in silence. As we walk to the car I want to tell her how glad I am that she's home and how nice it is to finally be having real conversations with her, but it sounds a little ridiculous and I'm too shy, so instead I link my arm through hers and hope that she is somehow able to sense all of the things I can't bring myself to say.

Turquoise Sea

The last thing I want to see after eating ice cream is the bathing suit I bought, but there it is, lying on the floor of my closet, taunting me, and suddenly I realize what I have to do. There's a town about forty miles away that I've driven through with my parents once or twice that has some spas and cute stores that sell things like healing crystals and Tibetan wind chimes. I feel like doing it there will be easier, more gentle somehow, and, after asking Sonia for some of the hundred bucks Dad gave her, I drive to the town, park in the municipal parking lot, and walk into the first spa I find, Mountain Sprite Spa and Massage.

There are two women in the waiting room, both of whom look up at me from their respective magazines when I walk in. They are, unlike me, no doubt here for the more "normal" spa services offered on the menu, like a Reiki healing massage or an ayurvedic facial.

"Can I help you?" The receptionist is old, like grandmother old, with a sagging neck and varicose veins on her hands. She's wearing a deep-turquoise-colored caftan and a turquoise beaded necklace, and her white hair is dyed an intense purple. I've never met anyone so old with purple hair. In fact, I've never even seen anyone with purple hair.

There are only about five feet between the chairs the customers are sitting in and the receptionist. I press my stomach against the desk and lean in toward her, but I can't bring myself to speak.

Funky Grandma holds up a brochure. She's also wearing a turquoise bracelet and a turquoise pinkie ring. I focus on the ring, bright blue in a silver setting, as I try to control my nerves. "Would you like to see a list of our services?" she asks.

Say it, Nina. "I'd like to get a back wax," I whisper. I'm torn between extreme relief that I've finally released those words into the world and the horror that someone else has now heard them.

"I'm sorry, you'd like what kind of wax?" Funky Grandma asks, turning her right ear toward me. Of course I had to find the only spa in upstate New York where the receptionist is hard of hearing.

I lean in farther, but this tactic doesn't work so well, because it only causes Funky Grandma to lean back. "I want to get a back wax," I whisper again, a little louder this time.

"You'd like to get your back waxed?" Funky Grandma repeats, loud enough that the two women behind me can't help but have heard. I don't ever want to have to turn around and face them.

What I want to do is crawl underneath Funky Grandma's chair and die, quickly, painlessly, in her sea of turquoise. I nod, and Funky Grandma nods. "Have a seat. It'll be about twenty minutes."

As I walk to one of the empty chairs I refuse to lift my eyes from the wood floor, and for the next twenty minutes I pretend to be completely absorbed in a magazine article about one woman's quest to find her birth parents.

"Ma'am?" A woman in a white shirt and pants smiles down at me. Her hair is not dyed an unusual color, but she does have a silver streak in it. "You can follow me," she says.

She leads me down a corridor into a small room, where there's a raised cushioned waxing bed next to a table. On the table are a metal container full of wax resting on something resembling a hot plate, some spatulas, and cloth strips. There's music playing in the background, melodic New Age–style music with a lot of flute. "You're here to have your back waxed?" she asks, like it's the most normal thing in the world.

"Yes," I say. She leaves the room so I can strip to my underwear. I lie on my stomach on top of the paper that covers the bed. When she returns I'm glad I'm lying on my stomach and can't see her reaction to my naked back. I'm facing a wall that has a framed quote by the Dalai Lama on it. It says, "Remember that not getting what you want is sometimes a wonderful stroke of luck."

"Let me know if it's too hot," the woman tells me, and the waxing begins. It's painful, but it isn't anything I can't handle. Both of us are silent as she works, and soon she's spreading lotion on my back and it's over and my stripe has been temporarily vanquished. "It'll be red for a little bit," the woman says before she leaves the room. I put my clothes on, hand thirty-five dollars to Funky Grandma, and get out of there as fast as I can.

The Curse of the Stripe

When I reach home I take a nap, and by the time I wake up the pain has ceased. I run to my full-length mirror to see how it looks. The stripe is gone, but my skin has reacted to the waxing in the worst possible way. It's covered in tiny, red, pimply bumps, as though my entire back came down with an awful case of chicken pox. There's no way I can ever wear the bathing suit I bought now.

I curse at my stripe, but really it's the other way around. It's as though it's protected by a version of Tutankhamun's curse: any attempt to remove this stripe will result in a terrible plague of pimples on your back. The only way I can get rid of it now is by electrolysis, which will take years and maybe even elicit a similarly horrid reaction.

All I can think of to do is cry, but after about five minutes of sobbing I realize that maybe this isn't the healthiest reaction. Yes, I'm hairy in a world where hair is considered unattractive on women. Yes, I will be stuck with my stripe for a while. But this is my body and this is who I am and feeling sorry for myself isn't going to change the situation, or make it any better. Why direct so much negative energy inward, at something you can't even help? I should reserve any negative energy for the things and people who really deserve it, like men who don't put the toilet seat down or people who drive on the shoulder to try to bypass bumper-to-bumper traffic. My name is Nina

Khan, and I'm a skunk girl. Right now my back looks like it has a novel written on it in Braille and I have to wear a T-shirt over my bathing suit, and this makes me a little different, yes, but not any less beautiful. Not one bit.

And Now, a Word from Ghalib

Helena calls the next morning. "Hello!" she chirps. "Are you awake?"

"I am now."

"I love mornings," she says. "New dawn, new day, new possibilities. Anyway, I was just calling to give you a little pep talk because I thought you might be nervous about seeing Asher."

"Actually, I feel pretty okay. I'm kind of nervous about getting on skis, but then I think of how Anthony's doing it and I feel better."

"That's wonderful! I guess you don't need my pep talk after all."

She sounds a little disappointed that there's no need for whatever speech that she's spent all of this time preparing. "Give it to me anyway," I tell her.

"Oh, I was going to tell you what happened when I first asked Asher to come skiing. I didn't mention you at first, and he said he couldn't come. And then I told him you were coming, and he said, 'Really?' and changed his mind right away. He was trying to hide it, but I could sense his excitement."

"He really seemed excited?"

"Indeed. And if that's not enough evidence that he likes you, then I don't know what is. Love is just around the corner, Nina. All you have to do is open up your heart to it," she says. "And you can stop rolling your eyes now."

"I'm not rolling my eyes. That's Bridget's department." After I hang up I wonder how exactly Helena knew that Asher was excited. Could she hear it stirring in his voice?

"What's up? You look a little too cheerful for this early in the morning," Sonia says when I come downstairs, already wearing my ski outfit since Bridget insisted that we go straight to the mountain to maximize our slope time. She's sitting cross-legged on a chair at the kitchen table, eating a bowl of cornflakes. "Is it because you're going to see Asher today?"

"I've decided I actually like being me," I explain. "That's huge for a teenager, right?"

She laughs. "It's a milestone, for sure."

"I feel pretty calm, but that might change when I see him."

"Ah, the trials of young love," Sonia says. "Not that it ever gets any easier." Then she recites something in Urdu that I don't understand.

"What did you just say?"

"Do you know who Ghalib is?"

"He's that famous Urdu poet."

"Right." Sonia nods. "He wrote this *ghazal* that basically says that although the pangs of love might be fatal, there's no way out of it, because if you didn't have those love pangs, your heart would just grieve over not having anything to grieve about."

"That's very apt, isn't it?" I say. "Since when do you read Urdu poetry?"

"I've been studying it in college," Sonia says. "Listen, Nina. I know this has been quite a week for you, and, as I said before, I don't want to tell you what to do, but I do want you to remember that life is about a lot more than parties and ski weekends. It's also about taking responsibility for your actions." Then she smiles at me, supercheerful, as if she just told a joke instead of dropping some weighty instruction onto my shoulders.

"Anything else, Polonius?"

"Very funny."

"I feel like you've set some high expectations for me," I tell her.

"Of course I have. You're my little sister." There's a honk outside. "There's your ride. Have fun." She opens up her arms. "A hug for the road."

We embrace for a second in a tight hug my father would be proud of. "See you tomorrow," I say, and she follows me to the front door, waving to my friends in the car.

"Good morning!" Helena says.

"Not feeling too nervous, are you?" Bridget asks, winking at me.

"I'm feeling quite calm," I tell them.

"You're calm?" Anthony says. "I'm frigging terrified."

"There's nothing to be terrified about, hot buns. We're just going to do the bunny slope over and over," Bridget reassures him.

"Bunnies can be terrifying," he counters. "On Grenada, we have killer rabbits. They attack tourists when they sleep, especially white girls who make their boyfriends do scary things."

"We should all go to Grenada," Helena says. "I've always fantasized about an island romance."

"With a killer bunny?" I joke.

"Yeah," Bridget adds. "Except he'd probably mistake Helena for a carrot and try to eat her."

"You know, Bridget," Helena says, "it's very lucky for you that I'm a lover, not a fighter."

"Speaking of lovers, where's Asher?" I ask.

"Why? Is your tongue getting impatient?" Bridget says.

I ignore this and Helena squeezes my hand. "He said he had to run some errands this morning. He's meeting us at the lodge." She shakes her head. "I can't believe that I'm going to be the fifth wheel."

"It'll be good for you," I tell her. "Experience how the other half lives."

"If I die, I want to be buried in my schwa sweatshirt," Anthony says.

"You're not going to die! It's going to be great," Bridget insists, and they start talking about what we're going to do and how Bridget's mom is making us her famous beef brisket for dinner and whether or not we should rent a horror movie, and I think about the Ghalib quote Sonia mentioned. I promise myself that no matter what happens, I won't regret the way I panged for Asher, because it has made my heart feel so alive.

One Enormous Step for Nina

Asher is waiting for us inside the lodge, in front of the ticket counter. Like Bridget, he's wearing professional gear: black ski pants, a yellow tinted pair of sunglasses hanging around his neck by a thick strap, and big black gloves clipped to his red-and-black ski jacket. I'm wearing track pants and a sweater and brought along these green gloves that are my father's but fit me pretty well since I have such big hands. "I'm really excited," he says to us. "I haven't been skiing since last winter."

He looks so cute. He looks like he was born on a mountain, though I bet he'd look just as great on a beach. His hotness has no geographical boundaries. I inhale, exhale, uncurl my toes. "How are you?" I ask him.

He smiles at me. "Now that exams are over, I'm great. How are you?"

"Excellent," I reply. Asher raises his eyebrows at this, probably because *excellent* is such a strong word, but that's exactly the impression I want to give. A strong word for a strong woman.

"Asher! Glad you could make it. We're going to have a great time tonight," Bridget says.

"Actually, I have to go back home this evening," Asher says. "A waiter called in sick at the restaurant and I have to cover his shift."

So much for a night away with Asher. I guess it was too good to be true.

"That's okay, you'll just have to make the most of today," Bridget says, and I hope she's not trying to send him a not-so-subliminal message. "All right, people, no more wasting time. Let's get our tickets!"

I've never seen Anthony so pale. "Anthony, get any more scared and you'll end up as white as Bridget," I tell him, but he's too nervous to appreciate the humor.

"I'm not skiing," Helena announces. "I'm going to spend the afternoon curled up in front of the lodge fireplace with a cup of hot cocoa and my Austria travel guide."

"Are you serious?" Bridget asks.

Helena nods. "I need to prepare for my trip. My mother and I are spending a weekend by ourselves in Vienna and I want to figure out what we should do."

Bridget turns to Anthony. "Don't get any ideas," she warns him. "You and I are hitting the bunny slope. We'll meet you guys back here at four."

I touch Anthony's arm and he turns around. "Don't be too scared," I tell him. "Didn't your grandmother say, 'A man isn't really a man until he faces his fears?' "

"No," Anthony says. "But thanks."

Bridget takes Anthony's arm and starts to pull him away. "I'll be sending you good vibes," she whispers to me.

And then there were three. "I'm going on a hunt for a leather armchair and a steaming cup of hot cocoa," Helena says. "Have a lovely day, you two."

And then there were two. Asher looks at me. "Shall we go have a lovely day?"

"I think *lovely* is about the last word you'd use to describe me on skis," I say.

"Don't ski much, I take it?"

"I'm pretty bad. I mean, I made it down a few blue squares, but I've never really gotten past the snow plow."

"That's okay," he says. "We'll take the lift up together and I'll wait for you at the bottom."

I'm thrilled that Asher wants to spend time with me, but this also means that he'll see what an oaf I am on skis. Asher waits as I get my lift ticket and rent my equipment. He seems anxious to get out in the snow, and I can't help but think that he wouldn't wait for me like this if he wasn't so keen on hanging out with me.

"Ready?" Asher asks as I approach, clanking in my boots. All of a sudden, I can't talk. I'm not that comfortable on a snowy mountain to begin with, and now here I am, on a snowy mountain with the boy I like. "I looked at the trail map, and there's a pretty easy slope that goes from the top of the mountain and winds its way down," he says. "Do you want to start with that?"

I nod, still unable to form words. I follow him outside and we put on our skis and he turns to me. "Should we take the high-speed lift or the slow one?" he asks.

This is a question that can't be answered with a mere nod. "Whichever you prefer."

"Let's take the slow one," he says. "We can enjoy the scenery."

I'm also in favor of the slow lift, since it means we'll have more time together, though the only scenery that I'll be enjoying is him. We get in line for the lift. It's a four-person lift and it's just the two of us waiting for the next one, but Asher stands right next to me. I'm always worried that when the chairlift approaches I'll somehow miss it and end up on my butt, but it's a smooth transition from standing to sitting. There's lots of space on either side of us, but he doesn't move over and neither do I. We're so close that it makes me too nervous to look at him. I'm hyperaware of the silence between us, of how slow the lift is moving, of the pressure of his arm against mine, of the bird flying in the air to my right.

"How did the rest of your finals go?" Asher asks me.

"Fine," I say. "What about you?"

"I think I did okay. I did the best I could anyway."

If I don't shift our conversation away from academics he'll think I have little else to talk about. "So, judging from how professional you look, I'm guessing you're a good skier."

"I guess you could say that."

"Where did you learn?"

"In the *Dolomiti*. They're part of the Alps," he says.

"They must have been much more impressive than this."

"This mountain isn't too bad," he says. "But it isn't too great, either."

"Listen, you really don't have to ski with me. I know you're longing for those double black diamonds."

"No," he replies. "I want to be here." He leans toward me a little, and our faces are so close I can see the tiny dark flecks in his irises. And I start willing him to kiss me, like I did before, except now I'm safely secured in a chairlift and can't possibly run away. Asher Richelli, you will kiss me. You will kiss me. The sun emerges from behind a cloud and the snow begins to sparkle. It has to be a sign.

Asher points to our right. "Did you see that guy wipe out?"

"No, I missed it."

"It looked painful. Serena told me about how she got into a skiing accident once. She wasn't too badly hurt, but it freaked her out so much she never went skiing again," he says.

"I didn't know that." Hearing Asher utter Serena's name has dulled even the brilliance of the sun.

"You two have never gotten along, have you?"

"We're better than we were before, I guess." And now that he's brought up Serena, I can't let it go. "The two of you seemed pretty intense together."

"Intense? Maybe. We only dated for two months," he says. "It didn't work out in the end, but she really helped me get used to a new school and a new place. She's not a bad person, Nina. And she's the only girl I've ever met who knows how to shear a llama." He looks at me with those brown eyes that are so soft, if they were pillows I would lay my head on them forever. "Are you holding the fact that I dated Serena against me?"

"No, but it is kind of weird."

"What's weird?" he asks.

That you could like someone like me when I'm so different from her. But I'd risk sounding presumptuous if I said that.

He elbows me. "What's weird?"

"Serena and I are really different, that's all."

He smiles. "I see."

"What do you see?" What I see is the end of the lift ahead of us, and I wish the mountain was twice as high, that this ride would never end. Asher doesn't say anything, and it's my turn to elbow him. "What do you see?"

Sometimes, things happen that are so fortuitous they can only have been caused by an act of Allah, or fate, or a guardian angel, or whatever. This sort of thing never happens to me, but suddenly, without warning, it does happen—the lift stops, and there we are, our bodies close together, suspended in the air.

"You're wondering how I could be interested in you when you're so different from Serena," he says.

He said it! He said he was interested in me! Okay, so he didn't say those exact words, but he definitely implied them. And then I realize that maybe this is an unfair question to pose, that maybe someone should be allowed to like two different people and not be asked to justify or feel bad about it. "You don't have to answer that," I say. "It's none of my business anyway." I'd like to ask him if he really, truly is interested in me, but I chicken out and change the topic altogether. "How's your mother doing?"

As soon as I mention his mother he frowns. "What's the matter? Is everything all right?" I ask.

"Oh, it's just that she's been complaining a lot recently. You know how much she hates Deer Hook. But my father says we have to stay, at least until I graduate next year, because the restaurant is doing well and he doesn't want me to change high schools a second time. And I don't want to leave, either. I feel bad that she's unhappy. The other night she was saying how she wants to spend all of next summer in Italy, but my father said he needed her help with the restaurant for part of it, and they got into this huge fight. But we should talk about happy things. How was Shannon's party?"

I roll my eyes. "I'm still recovering."

"I heard you passed out under a tree or something?"

"How do you know that?"

"Deer Hook is a small town," he says. "If Nina Khan shows up to a party and passes out, word gets around."

"That's so weird."

"What is?"

"That people were talking about something I did. I'm never a topic of conversation—at least not in that way."

"It was your first high school party, right?"

I nod. "My first, and my last."

"Well, I wish I had been there. Sounds like you really made a splash."

"More like a thump," I say. He laughs, and there's a gentleness to it that makes me want to throw my arms around him.

"How were you able to go to Shannon's party anyway? I'm pretty sure it wasn't because of what I said to your parents when you guys came to the restaurant," he says, grinning.

I laugh. "No, not quite. My parents are already in Pakistan. My sister and I are leaving Monday."

"That's going to be a great experience, don't you think?"

I nod. "It should be. Imagine hearing so much about a place, eating its food, wearing its clothes, celebrating its holidays, spending a lot of time with people from there, but never actually seeing it. Now I'll finally be able to put a face to the name, you know?"

He smiles his lopsided smile, and it's the perfect time for me to lean in and kiss him. I tell myself, You can do it, you can do it, but the lift starts again and the moment has passed. We're both quiet and the bird that was flying to our right suddenly dives toward the snow like it's mistaken it for an ocean.

We ski down a miniature slope together, and then Asher does a quick 180-degree turn so that we're facing each other. "This is the easy trail I was talking about," he says, pointing at it with his pole. "I thought I'd go down it with you this time. I'll let you get a head start."

The last thing I want is for Asher to stand at the top and watch me ski. "You should go first."

"It's okay, I really don't mind," he says.

It's hopeless. I look at the trail. It's wide and not too steep and it seems to wind a lot, which is good. All I need to do is take it easy, one ski at a time. But as I start to ski I keep thinking of how Asher is behind me, observing my skill, or, rather, lack thereof, and instead of skiing the way I usually do, which is to go down the trail in horizontal crisscross motions so I don't go too fast, I keep my skis parallel and go straight down. And then the wind is at my back and I tuck my poles underneath my arms like you see racers do and I'm speeding down the mountain. It's exhilarating until I realize that I'm going too fast and there's no way I'll be able to stop and this was a stupid, stupid idea. There's another skier in front of me who I'm on a collision course with and behind me I can hear Asher yelling for me to slow down. I try to execute a turn and end up performing some kind of split, poles in the air. Luckily, I wipe out away from the other skiers, near the edge of the trail, my face in the snow, one of my skis a little ways down the mountain from me.

"Are you okay?" Asher asks, skiing up to me.

"I'm fine," I lie. I'm mortified.

Asher retrieves my ski and sidesteps up the mountain with it. "Are you sure you're okay? That fall looked painful."

I rub my butt, which I know is going to be bruised tomorrow. Could I be a bigger idiot? Has the weight of these boots somehow drained the intelligence from my brain? "I usually don't ski like that."

"Good," he says. "Because you could get yourself hurt." He takes his skis off and kneels down next to me. "You weren't trying to impress me, were you?"

"If I was I failed miserably."

"I don't know," he says. "That split thing you did was pretty impressive."

"Sorry, but the Nina Khan show is officially over. There will be no repeat performance."

He laughs. "Are you going to put those skis back on or what?"

"I have an idea. Let's forget about skiing," I say. I lie back in the snow and stretch my arms out. "Let's make lots of snow angels and then go drink hot cocoa in front of the fire."

Asher shakes his head. "First skiing, then hot cocoa," he says. I stick my tongue out at him. "All right." He lies down next to me. "One snow angel for the lady."

We make back-and-forth movements with our hands and legs, our feet meeting for a brief second. The sun is shining with full force and we lie there in silence, enjoying the warmth on our skin. Asher sits up, so I do too, and we stay this way, watching as people ski past us.

"I love mountains," he says. "When I was young I was so fascinated by them. My father bought me this book about mountaineers and I think I read it, like, a hundred times, and every time I read it I felt like putting on my boots and exploring the world. One time I actually did put my boots on and leave my house, but when I got to the end of our block I got scared and ran right back home."

"I can relate," I say. "I used to play this game where I'd put my finger on the globe and spin it and wherever it landed was going to be my future home."

"What if it landed on the ocean?"

"I'd spin it again. I remember after my parents bought me a

stuffed kangaroo, for a while I would spin and spin it until I landed on Australia."

"Australia," Asher repeats. "I've always wanted to go there."

"Me too," I say, and I feel it, the possibility of it, Asher and me, a few years from now maybe, running into each other in front of the opera house in Sydney, gazing into each other's eyes, surprise turning to gratitude turning to love.

"Nina?" Asher says. "Can I ask you something?"

"Sure."

"Why did you run away from me that day?"

Oh, no. How best to explain this? Helena would respond by saying something about how she was overwhelmed with emotion, and Bridget would respond with some wisecrack, and me? "I freaked out," I tell him.

"Why? Because of your parents?"

"It's complicated," I say. "A little bit because of my parents, and a little bit because—" I make fists in the snow. "A little bit because I like you."

"I like you too," he says, and then he takes my hand.

And I start laughing. I don't mean to laugh, but I'm so happy and scared and surprised that I can't help it.

"Why are you laughing?"

"It's so crazy that you like me."

"Why?"

"I don't know," I say. "Because I'm a dork."

"Why wouldn't I like you? You're pretty and you're smart and you make me laugh, and whenever I talk to you, I feel like I could tell you anything and you'd understand. And you're not afraid to do your own thing. I really admire that about you." He shrugs. "But maybe you're right—I mean, who would ever like a dork?"

I shake my head. "Certainly not you."

"Certainly not," he says, and then his head starts moving toward me and he's coming in fast, like he's a rocket and I'm the gravitational pull, and I close my eyes and try to remain calm. Then his lips land on mine and swish back and forth a bit, until I remember that I'm supposed to part my lips, so I do and here we are, kissing on top of a snowy mountain, then we pull away and I'm looking into his eyes and I can't stop smiling and neither can he.

I've been kissed! One enormous step for Nina, one irrelevant step for mankind.

"So we both like each other," he says, tracing my cheekbone with his finger. "What do you think we should do about it?"

I was hoping he'd hold off on that, that he wouldn't bring up the future, because all I want to do is stay with the now, with Asher and me in the shimmering snow, for as long as possible. "I don't know," I tell him. Except I do know. I'm just not ready to say it.

"What are you thinking?" he asks.

How do I explain? I've been allowing myself to indulge in fantasies unfettered by responsibilities or repercussions, because what's the point of considering those things when you're still in the realm of wishful thinking? But now, here is my wish come true, and here is its companion, consequence, and it's time to face them both. "My parents leave the country," I begin, "and suddenly I'm Cinderella, going to parties and ski trips, and—and kissing you. But it's not like you're going to show up at my house with a glass slipper and we will live happily ever after."

"I think I see where you're going with this," he says.

"What would we do—have a relationship confined to the walls of our school, and maybe a few other stolen moments? I'd sneak down to the basement in the middle of the night so I could talk to you on the phone? You deserve to be with a girl who can be with you completely. And I, I can't." It's not as difficult to say this as I thought it would be, but I know this isn't the most difficult part; that's going to be later, when I have to watch Asher go out with some other girl, and remember how, for a few brilliant hours, he was mine.

"I understand," he says. He wipes a tear from my cheek; I hadn't even realized I was crying. "I wouldn't want you to do anything you weren't totally comfortable with."

"I'm sorry," I tell him. "If my situation was different—"

"Then you wouldn't be Nina," he says. He puts his hand under my chin. "I'm still really glad I came today. Aren't you?"

I nod and he tilts my face up and we kiss again. We kiss for what must be a few minutes but seems like hours. Oh, how we kiss.

It's me who pulls away first. "We probably shouldn't be hanging out at the edge of a ski trail," I say.

"This is true," he says, helping me up. We put our skis back on, but neither of us moves.

"You should go ahead." I want to be alone because I know I'm going to cry a little more, as much from joy as from sadness.

"But what if you fall?"

"I won't."

"How about this," he says. "I'll keep stopping and wait for you to catch up with me before I go again."

"Deal." We stand there for a second, neither of us knowing quite what to say. How do you commemorate the end of a moment? "I'll see you in a bit," he says, and then he's off, zigzagging down the trail with an agility I could only dream of.

There's just one thin cloud on the horizon and the sky is deep blue. This is my first time at the top of a mountain, and the skiers and the lodge and the cars in the parking lot seem so tiny, and I picture all of the people I care about, in miniature. There's Asher, gracefully mastering the snow, and there are Bridget and Anthony on the bunny slope, and there is Helena, curled up in the lodge, dreaming of a Vienna romance, and, farther away, there's Sonia at home with her nose in some book, and, even farther than that, there are my parents in Pakistan, reuniting with the place they once called home. And then there's me, Nina Khan, who is leaving her fairy-tale summit and beginning her descent, slow and steady and confident, because this time, she plans on making it without falling down.

Karachi

The flight to Karachi is the longest I've ever taken. Sonia sleeps most of the way. It's easy for her to sleep on planes. I pass the time reading and thinking about my kiss with Asher, but something about being on a plane that is heading toward a different hemisphere makes remembering what it actually felt like more and more difficult. By the time we land, I've stopped trying to relive my first kiss and have accepted that it's over, that it's become a memory, but one I can cherish and hold close to my heart for as long as I'd like.

When we pull up to the gate in Karachi, everyone immediately rises, stretching their arms and legs. The plane is buzzing with the talk and laughter of aunties and uncles and grandparents and children of all ages and the energy is contagious. Even though I've barely slept I suddenly feel wide awake.

The airport looks brand-new. It's modern and has marble floors and large windows that look out onto the tarmac. Sonia and I stop by the bathroom to brush our teeth and our hair, as per our mother's instructions, then take our place in the foreign visitors' line. The passport official's lips are an unnatural shade of red, probably from eating too much betel nut. "Your first time in Pakistan?" he asks, peering at us over his gold-rimmed glasses.

"Yes," Sonia says softly, like it's a confession, and for a second I wonder if he could deny us entry simply because we waited so long to come.

"Welcome," he says, handing us back our passports.

The scene outside the airport is chaotic. Just as Ma said, the coolies descend upon us as soon as we exit the baggage claim area. We keep a tight grip on our luggage cart and keep telling them no. They're all men, mostly skinny, and it's impressive to watch them pick up large suitcases and hoist them onto their shoulders. There are passengers arriving and departing and people dropping them off or picking them up and coolies running around and people who just seem to be loitering, and there's a man who's asleep, slumped against a column, and there's a police officer and a few beggars, including one who's missing a leg and a hand and is on crutches. Sonia gives him some of the rupees Dad left for us, and we scan the crowd, trying to find our parents.

I've never seen anything like this, or smelled air so heavy with a musk that's like a mixture of spices and pollution. Everything seems strange, yet, at the same time, it's somehow familiar, like I've been here before but I've misplaced the memory.

"Can you believe this place?" Sonia says. "How are they going to be able to find us?"

And then we spot our parents, across the crowd. Sonia and I wave and they wave back and start to make their way toward us. There are Ma and Dad and Nasreen Khala and Khalu and their daughters who look much older than I remember and all of these people I don't know, including two cute twin girls with their hair in braids, clutching red roses that I'm guessing are for us. I'm touched that so many of them have come to meet us at the airport at this predawn hour, though I have no idea how I'm going to learn all of their names.

Sonia turns to me. "Ready?" she says.

"I'm ready," I reply. We push our luggage carts forward, heading into the crowd to meet our family halfway. I'm happy to see my parents and a little bit nervous about meeting everyone else. But, most of all, I'm excited, because here begins a whole new adventure, and who knows what could happen next?

Acknowledgments

The first person I must acknowledge is Kevin Brockmeier—if he hadn't decided to teach a children's fiction workshop my first semester at Iowa, the book might never have been written. I'd also like to thank my agent, Ayesha Pande, for believing in this book from the beginning; my editor, Janine O'Malley, for her wisdom and guidance and for never losing sight of the emotional heart of the book; Caryl Pagel and Danny Khalastchi, for being such wonderful readers; and Rahim Rahemtulla, just for being there. I am grateful to my family for their support and, most of all, to Faisal, for all of his love and encouragement, every step of the way.